從身旁事物開始學習的

生活英語

三民英語編輯小組　譯

古藤 晃 (KOTOH Koh)
河合補習班講師。
專為社會人士及應考學生所設
立的「日曜講座」主持人。目
前，正全心投入嶄新概念的辭
典編纂工作中。已有多冊英語
學習的相關著作問世。

〰〰 三民書局

國家圖書館出版品預行編目資料

從身旁事物開始學習的生活英語 / 古藤晃著;三民英語編
輯小組譯.－－二版二刷.－－臺北市；三民，2018
　　面；　公分

　ISBN 978-957-14-5576-1　（平裝）
　1. 英語 2. 會話

805.188　　　　　　　　　　　　　　　　100018510

© 從身旁事物開始學習的生活英語

編 著 者	古藤晃
譯　　者	三民英語編輯小組
發 行 人	劉振強
著作財產權人	三民書局股份有限公司
發 行 所	三民書局股份有限公司
	地址　臺北市復興北路386號
	電話　(02)25006600
	郵撥帳號　0009998-5
門 市 部	(復北店) 臺北市復興北路386號
	(重南店) 臺北市重慶南路一段61號
出版日期	初版一刷　2000年5月
	二版一刷　2014年2月
	二版二刷　2018年5月
編　　號	S 803020

行政院新聞局登記證局版臺業字第○二○○號

有著作權‧不准侵害

ISBN　978-957-14-5576-1　（平裝）

http://www.sanmin.com.tw　三民網路書店

※本書如有缺頁、破損或裝訂錯誤，請寄回本公司更換。

Original material: © Koh KOTOH, 1999
This translation of *English Vocabulary for Daily Life* originally
published in Japanese in 1999 is published by arrangement with
Kenkyusha publishing Co., Ltd.

　　增強英語能力的方法不勝枚舉，或許大家都已經試遍了各種覺得可行的方案，卻成效不彰。其實，還是有許多能讓學習變得更為有趣的方法，其中之一就是單字，也就是從名詞開始著手，尤其是從身旁的「事物」開始，學習這些事物在英文中的說法，進而瞭解它們在日常英文中的表現。如此一來，不僅藉由實際生活中的不斷運用，這些生活周遭的用語能自然地留在腦海裡，而且也是成效頗佳的英語學習法。

　　但是，在我們學習英語之前，有些事情必須特別注意。

　　其一就是，有些詞彙根本是實際生活中不會使用的「英語」。我們的身旁充斥著過多的假性英語詞彙，就以電影或電視等深具代表性的媒體來說，特別是商業廣告中經常可見使用大量的外來語。若不細心加以區別，其頻繁的程度幾乎已經到了讓人誤以為在美國或英國也是這麼用的，但是其中卻夾雜了相當比例的日式英語。這樣的英語除了日本人之外，外國人是無法理解的，相信對於 native speaker 而言也會覺得非常奇怪。

　　此外，即使是我們認為與日文具有相同語義的英文單字，若經仔細推敲的話，將會發現彼此之間依然存在著概念上或語義上細微的不同。或是日文既有的語彙在英文中缺乏相對應的用法，或是正好相反，雙方都僅有單方存在的獨特語彙。在您深入閱讀本書之後將不難發現，即使是身旁的事物中也不乏這樣的例子。

　　英美和日本，當然是歷史和文化截然不同的兩個世界，無可避免的，有時也會因為完全迥異的文化背景而造成對異文化的理解停留在較淺的層面，因而有許多牛頭不對馬嘴的對話產生。

若對英文的學習有著重新來過 (brush up) 的想法，就更應該記誦正確的表現方式。像有些人因為求學或工作等原因必須開始在海外生活，若不知道正確的表現方式，恐怕連攸關性命的時候，也難以自救。光是學些自以為瞭解的英語不僅幫不上忙，可能還會為你帶來麻煩呢！

本書完全以上述問題為鑑，除了以日常生活中隨處可見的各種物品為媒介，並以讀者諸君能自其中習得正確表現為編輯的方向，對於內容做了許多獨特的規劃，大致的架構如下所示。

首先，大致分為 indoor 和 outdoor 兩大部分，將我們日常接觸的許多場景帶入其中。indoor 的部分設定為「屋內篇」，包含客廳、廚房、浴室等生活不可或缺的場景。outdoor 的部分則設定為「屋外篇」，其中包含了由學校到便利商店等年輕學子們經常出入的行動範圍。此外，也將交通工具、汽車、飛機等另外設定了「外出篇」加以解說。

各個場景的內容，基本上由以下四個部分組成。

Vocabulary	首先，先記憶生活中會使用到的單字吧。
用英語說說看	試著運用之前學過的 vocabulary 造造句子。
你應該要知道	告訴你關於詞彙的深層意含。
須注意的英語	詳細的解說加強你對英文的語感。

雖然內容非常瑣碎，但是藉由一個一個地學習這些身旁的詞彙，慢慢地，希望能將讀者帶領到英語的境地裡，因而決定這樣的架構。雖然說這樣的架構並不是十分完備的，但這樣的內容至少已能引領讀者來到英文學習的入口，相信大家也必能從中有所學習才是。衷心地期望大家能輕鬆愉快地閱讀本書。

大家都知道，以英國為主的英語和以美國為主的英語在表

現上有時並不相同。即便是日常所使用的物品，不一樣的地方也比我們想像中來得多。本書中特地將英式表現以加註＊的方式標出，請多加注意。

　　本書的出版，若無以下三人的鼎力相助無法付梓。非常感謝為我細心校對英式表現的 Yamada Keito 先生、指導我英文的 Susan Capulan 女士及為我繪製可愛插圖的黑須和清先生，謹在此向他們表達我誠摯的謝意。

古藤　　晃

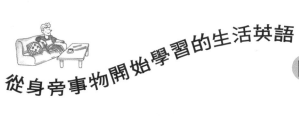

從身旁事物開始學習的生活英語

目次

屋內篇　1

住宅	2	浴室	32
玄關	10	客廳	40
廚房	16	庭院	48
垃圾	28	雜貨	56

屋外篇　61

| 購物 | 62 | 速食 | 76 |
| 便利商店 | 70 | 辦公室 | 80 |

電話	86
學校	90
銀行	96

郵局	100
美容院	104

外出篇 109

道路	110
汽車	120
交通工具	124

飛機	132
旅館	136

索 引 142

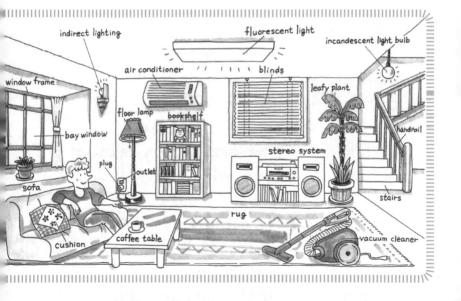

indirect lighting

fluorescent light

incandescent light bulb

air conditioner

blinds

leafy plant

window frame

floor lamp

bookshelf

handrail

bay window

stereo system

plug

outlet

stairs

sofa

vacuum cleaner

cushion

coffee table

rug

住宅

臺灣的住宅和歐美的相較之下常顯得寒酸。舉例來說，美國人在談到房子的大小時，不僅包含庭院，而且以畝為單位。他們通常說：「那棟房子有兩畝大」或是「我們家只有半畝大」。但是，一畝可是有 124 坪耶！

Vocabulary

公寓	apartment, *flat
	(整個建築物) an apartment house
	*a block of flats
套房	one-room apartment
	*bedsit, studio flat
分戶出售的公寓	condominium
社區	housing development, apartment complex
雙層建築	a two-story [*storey] building
內附家具	furnished
房租	rent
押金	deposit, security deposit
保證金	key money
頭期款	down payment
房屋貸款	housing loan, mortgage
抵押／擔保	mortgage, *security, collateral
車庫	garage, parking space

用英語說說看

❶ 我家是新蓋的。
My home is new.
I live in a brand-new house.

❷ 我家離最近的車站走路 10 分鐘。
My place [house] is a 10-minute walk from the nearest station.

❸ 我住在一棟 9 層樓建築的 5 樓。
I live on [I'm on] the 5th floor of a 9-story [*storey] building.

❹ 我正在找有附家具的公寓。
I'm looking for a furnished apartment [*flat].

❺ 押金要多少錢呢？
How much is the deposit?

❻ 房貸使生活艱困。
Finances are tight with the housing loan [mortgage].
Things are difficult while paying off the housing loan [mortgage].

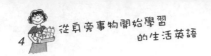

居住者	occupant, tenant
不動產業者	real estate agent [agency]
	*estate agent
契約重訂	contract renewal
木造	wooden, made of wood
鋼筋混凝土	ferroconcrete (ferro- (鐵的) + concrete)
向南	southern exposure, *south-facing
向陽	sunny, well-lit
在屋角的房間	a corner room, *room on the end of an apartment block
管理人	superintendent [略作 super]
	concierge ☞雖為法文，但在英語世界裡亦可通用。
	*building supervisor, caretaker
會議室	meeting house, assembly room
避難場所	evacuation point
獨棟的房子	free-standing house, single-family house, *detached house
鄉村風格的	country-style, rustic
別墅	second home, country home [house]

❶今晚 7 點開始在社區的會議室有個集會。

There will be a general meeting from 7:00 p.m. tonight in the meeting room of the apartment complex.

❷一個人住在獨棟的房子是很危險的。

Living alone in a free-standing house [*detached house] is dangerous.

三房二廳

若要解釋三房二廳的話，可以以下列方式說明。

Most apartments are built based on the following structural design: a kitchen, living space, and then one, two, or three rooms. Thus a 3LDK is an apartment with a large Living + Dining-Kitchen space and 3 other rooms. Cheaper apartments are lacking the living-dining space and go by 1K meaning one room plus a kitchen.

大部分的公寓會依以下的結構設計而興建：一間廚房、一塊活動的空間、外加一到三間房。3LDK 指的是有一間寬闊的客廳及餐廳、廚房，並有三間房間的公寓。更便宜的公寓則沒有客廳及餐廳的 1K，指的是僅有一間房間外加廚房的小套房。

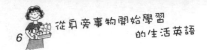

樓梯	(屋內) stairs, stairway, (屋外) steps
扶手	handrail, railing, banister, balustrade
樓梯中間的平臺	landing
通風處	open hallway, open stairwell
雙層窗戶	double window, *double glazing
百葉窗	window shade, *blind
凸窗	bay window
窗框	window frame
窗戶清潔	window cleaning, (人) window washer
重新裝潢	redecorate
閣樓	attic, loft
地下室	(用來住人的) basement
	(用來儲存物品的) cellar
儲藏室	(屋內) storage space
	(屋外) storage shed
倉庫	(家裡的置物櫃) closet
	(儲藏室) storeroom
	(屋外收藏東西的小屋) shed
	(擺放工具的小屋) tool house
空氣調節設備	air conditioning ☞主要指冷氣之意。
暖氣設備	heating
中央暖氣系統	central heating
廚房後門	back door, kitchen door

❶ 樓梯很陡，請多加小心。

The stairs are steep, so please be careful [take care].

❷ 路旁的窗戶為隔絕噪音而採用雙層窗戶。

The windows facing the street [road] are double windows [*double-glazed] to keep out noise.

❸ 閣樓被用來當作倉庫。

The attic is used as a storeroom.

❹ 空調設備適用於一年四季。

Combined heating and air conditioning units cover all seasons.

❺ 請從 (廚房) 後門進來。

Come in by the kitchen door [back door].

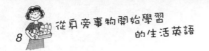
你應該要知道

住宅的樣式

[美式住宅] ranch house, rambler (平房)；colonial style (殖民地時期風格的建築。一、二樓幾乎相同大小，一樓為客廳、廚房等，寢室或浴室多在二樓。)

Cape Cod style (海岬風格的建築。一樓比二樓寬廣的別墅。)；split-level style (每個房間的樓板有高有低的建築。)

Spanish style (西班牙風格的建築。白灰泥的牆壁搭配紅色的屋頂，在南加州非常常見。)

美式住宅的樣式以地名命名的居多。

[英式住宅] 英式住宅的樣式則如 Elizabethan, Tudor, Victorian, Georgian, Edwardian Regency (攝政時代) 等，以各個時代命名的居多。

須注意的英語

◎ mansion

mansion 的原意是指有錢人住的大房子。

◎ key 和 lock

lock 為插入 key 的鑰匙孔。

◎ step 和 flight

step 指的是「樓梯的一階」，它的複數 steps 則為「樓梯」的意思。flight 是指「一段樓梯」，樓梯之間若有平臺的話，到平臺為止的一段樓梯稱作 a flight of stairs。此外，我們稱逃生梯為 fire escape。

◎ verandah 和 balcony 和 porch 和 deck

verandah 和 balcony 通常指二樓以上的陽臺。porch 和 deck 則指位於地面上的。一樓鋪設了地板，放置了椅子、桌子的側邊陽臺通常稱作 porch 而不用 deck。在英國，porch 指的是向外延伸的門廊。

◎ time sharing

將渡假村的某一段特定的時期 (例如只有盛夏的四個禮拜等)，以優惠的價格租用的型態。

◎ utility room

放置洗衣機、吸塵器、暖氣機等家電設備的房間。

玄關

正門是一個家的門面所在，更是接待附近鄰居、親朋好友等最重要的地方，雖然做好家居安全是很重要的，但是千萬也要注意不要損害溫暖的氣氛。

Vocabulary

門	gate
門柱	gate post
門牌、戶名牌	doorplate, nameplate
信箱	mailbox, *letter box
投郵口	(門上的投遞口) mail slot, mail drop, *letter box
車庫	garage ☞注意發音及重音。美式發音為 [gəˋrɑʒ]。英式發音為 [ˋgærɑʒ]。
大門口的臺階	front stairs [steps]
門口的燈	entrance light, entryway light, hall light, outside light
門鈴	doorbell
對講機	intercom, door phone
自動上鎖的門	auto lock, self-locking door
密碼	secret code, secret number
保安服務	security, burglar alarm, *house alarm
鎖鏈	chain lock, *security lock

◎用英語說說看

❶大門口的門牌有點歪。

The doorplate [nameplate] is slightly crooked.

❷在你進來之前看一下信箱。

Look in the mailbox [Check the mail] before you come up.

❸大門口的燈閃爍不定，請幫我看一下。

The entryway light [The hall light] is flickering. Please take a look (at it).

❹按下房間的號碼，然後按通話鈕。

Push (the buttons for) the room number, then push the intercom button.

❺這扇門的鎖很難打開 [生鏽了／卡住了]。

The lock on this gate is hard to open [rusted/stiff].

❻確認門有上鎖。

Make sure the door is locked.

Make sure you locked the door.

❼等一下！我有鎖門嗎？

Wait a minute! Did I lock the door?

後門	back door
廚房後門	kitchen door
門口的墊子	doormat
金屬刮泥片	door scraper
鞋拔	shoehorn
掛衣架	coat hanger, coat rack, *coat rail
畫	picture, painting
花瓶	vase

☞注意發音。美式發音為 [ves]。英式發音為 [vɑs]。

花	flowers
	(插花) flower arrangement
進門後供脫鞋的區域	area immediately inside the door for taking off shoes before entering into the house
私人車道	driveway
守衛	guard

☞在英國相當罕見。

鞋箱	shoe box, *shoe rack
傘架	umbrella stand
探視孔	peephole
門擋	doorstop
備份鑰匙	duplicate key, spare key

❶ 在你進門前，請把鞋子 (上的泥) 擦一擦。

Wipe your shoes (on the mat) before you come in.

❷ 進門前請脫鞋。

Please remove [take off] your shoes before coming in.

❸ 在你開門之前要先確認門外是誰。

Check who it is [who's there] before you open the door.

❹ 包裹應該今天就會送到。

The package should arrive sometime today.

❺ 你有包裹。／我這有一個你的包裹。

You have a package.

I have a delivery for you.

❻ 回來或出門，請都知會警衛一聲。

Let the guard know when you come in and go out.

❼ 打份備用鑰匙吧。

Let's make a duplicate [spare] key.

❽ 好像有人來，我去看看。

It looks [sounds] like someone's here [someone is at the door]. I'll go see [check].

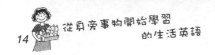

從身旁事物開始學習
的生活英語

你應該要知道

鞋子和拖鞋

通常在英國或美國，習慣上進入家門是不脫鞋的。這一點和我們的情形有所不同。

我們的習慣一般以玄關分內外，所以有的拜訪者自行開門的行為亦被容許。但是在英國或美國，通常必須站在門外等待，對於不熟識的人家，擅自開啟大門可是會挨告的。不過，有某些住家，其正門前的門廊 (porch) 也有等同玄關的功能。例如，在英國的農家就有在 porch 脫鞋入內的習慣。

由於大部分的情況都是不脫鞋的，所以為了去除鞋底沾黏的泥沙，在門口鋪設有 doormat。但是如果鞋子真的很髒，通常還是會脫掉。

至於 slippers 是指從早上起床到外出前這段期間在室內所穿的拖鞋。

到別人家拜訪的人通常利用 front door，但是家人或親密的朋友則通常會利用 back door。有的住家可以直接從 back door 進入 kitchen。有的則可以從 outbuilding (附屬建築) 或 utility room (用來放置洗衣機和 freezer 等的房間) 進入。

須注意的英語

◎ box

letter box 是指自己家裡用來收信、報紙的信箱。postbox 則指寄信的郵筒。但在美國則無此區分，兩者都稱作 mailbox。

在英國，shoe box 是指買鞋時隨鞋附贈的厚紙盒，放在玄關的「鞋架」通常稱作 shoe rack。但是，有很多家庭都不在玄關放置鞋架。

◎ steps 和 stairs

steps 大多指屋外的樓梯，stairs 則指建築物內部的樓梯。在英國或美國因正門的樓梯多在屋外，所以正確的譯法應該是 front steps。此外，英式住宅通常有正門通往二樓的樓梯，則譯作 hall stairs。

廚房

　　現代的廚房是依歐美的形式所設計的，除了有方便的烹飪器具及餐具外，也有合理的水管線路，是非常方便工作的廚房。但是，因為生活型態的不同，歐美廚房的規模通常較大。

Vocabulary

冷藏室	refrigerator [略作 fridge]
冷凍室	freezer
製冰盤	ice tray
洗碗機	dishwasher
廚架	shelf
餐具櫥	(架設在廚房的) cupboard
	(單獨的) cabinet
	(放在餐廳裡的) sideboard
烤箱	oven
微波爐	microwave (oven)
溫控轉鈕	temperature control, temperature knob
瓦斯	gas ☞美國使用瓦斯的家庭非常少，大部分都用電。
電磁爐	electromagnetic cooker ☞英國幾乎沒有。
瓦斯爐	(gas) burner
抽油煙機	(ventilation) fan, *extractor fan

🔧用英語說說看

❶請從冰箱拿出牛奶。

Please take the milk out of the fridge.

❷檢查一下冰箱並列出一張購買清單，可以嗎？

Check in the fridge and make a shopping list, OK?

❸冰箱裡有冰淇淋。

There's some ice cream in the freezer.

❹請把用過的餐具放入洗碗機。

Please put the dirty dishes into the dishwasher.

❺我搆不到架子的最上層，請幫我把那個大碗拿下來。

I can't reach the top shelf. Take [Get down] that big bowl for me.

❻請把烤箱預熱。

Please warm up the oven.

❼請用微波爐把它加熱 1 分鐘。

Please warm it up in the microwave for one minute.

❽抽油煙機上的污垢越早除去越好。

It's best to get rid of any dirt on the fan as quickly as possible.

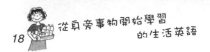

水壺	kettle
鍋子	(總稱) pots and pans
	(淺鍋) pan
	(深鍋) pot
	(壓力鍋) pressure cooker
燉鍋	saucepan, stew pot
長柄有蓋的深鍋	milk pan, small saucepan
煎鍋	frying pan
中式炒菜鍋	wok, Chinese frying pan
蒸籠	steamer
烤鍋、焙鍋	(陶器或玻璃製品) casserole
量杯	measuring cup
量匙	measuring spoons
食物保溫盤	hot plate
附有電湯匙的水壺	electric pot
濾過式咖啡壺	percolator
蓋子／把手／出水口	lid, handle, spout
果汁機	blender, *liquidizer
食物處理器	food processor
砧板	cutting board, chopping board
菜刀	kitchen knife, cooking knife
	☞cleaver 為大型的切肉刀。
水果刀	fruit knife, paring knife

❶ 我找不到量杯 [量匙]。

I can't find the measuring cup [spoons].

☞ 我們的 1 cup 指的是 200 cc，美國的大約是 240 cc (8 盎司)。spoon 則沒有差別，同樣是一茶匙 (1 teaspoon) 為 5 cc，一大匙 (1 tablespoon) 為 15 cc。

❷ 請秤 200 公克麵粉、100 公克奶油。

Please measure out 200 g of flour and 100 g of butter.

☞ 美國的食譜 (recipe) 中不以公克為單位，麵粉 (flour) 的話通常以 cups 為單位，奶油 (butter) 的話則以 tablespoon 為單位。

英國雖漸漸也使用公克，但是對年長的人來說，磅 (lb.) 及盎司 (oz.) 還是他們較為熟悉的。一公斤約等於 2.2 磅，一磅為 16 盎司。

❸ 這臺果汁機買得很划算。

This blender was a real deal [great bargain].

❹ 奶油好像用完了。

It looks like we're out of butter.

It looks like we've run out of butter.

❺ 水果刀在哪裡？

Where's the paring knife [fruit knife]?

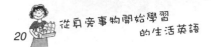

瓶子	bottle, (廣口瓶) jar
金屬罐	canister
餐具	dishes, (陶器) crockery
金屬餐具	cutlery
調味料	seasoning, spices
罐頭	canned food, *tinned food
開罐器	can opener, *tin opener
盤子	(大盤子) dish, (分取的盤子) plate
餅乾壓模	cookie cutter
打蛋器	eggbeater, *egg whisk
擀麵棍	rolling pin
碗	bowl
篩子	sieve
銼菜板	grater
開瓶器	(開瓶蓋用) bottle opener
	(開瓶塞用) corkscrew
鍋鏟	spatula
杓子	ladle
削皮器	peeler
檸檬榨汁器	lemon juicer, lemon squeezer
夾鉗	tongs
濾茶網	tea strainer
瀝水籃	drainer, strainer, *colander

❶ 請在餐桌上擺好餐具。
Please lay the table.

❷ 你能打開這個罐頭嗎？但請小心不要割傷自己。
Could you open that can, but be careful not to cut yourself?

❸ 當你用完調味料，要把蓋子蓋緊並排放整齊。
When you have finished with the seasonings, put the lids back on firmly and put them away.

❹ 用擀麵棍將麵糰擀開後，用你喜歡的模型切出各種形狀。
After rolling out the cookie dough with a rolling pin, cut out any shapes you like with the cookie cutters.

❺ 把鮮奶油放入碗中，用電動攪拌器打到發泡為止。
Put the fresh cream in a bowl and whisk with an electric whisk until it forms peaks.

❻ 我找不到開瓶器，有誰知道在哪裡？
I can't find the corkscrew, does anyone know where it is?

❼ 這削皮器很方便使用。
This peeler is very easy to use.

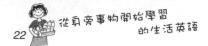

餐墊	place mat, *luncheon mat
蠟紙	waxed paper, *greaseproof paper
保鮮膜	plastic wrap, (商品名) Saran Wrap, *cling film
鋁箔紙	(aluminum) foil
紙巾	paper napkin, *serviette
廚房水槽	kitchen sink
淨水裝置	water purifier
水龍頭	faucet, *tap
排水溝	(屋內) drain
	(屋外) gutter
海綿	sponge
刷子	brush
鬃毛刷子	stiff brush, scouring brush
洗滌劑	dish detergent, *washing-up liquid
肥皂	soap
廚房用紙巾	paper towel, *kitchen roll
抹布	dishrag, dishcloth
餐具籃	dish drainer, drainer tray
垃圾桶	trash can, garbage can, *rubbish bin

❶ 我們喝的是礦泉水 (而不是自來水)。

We drink mineral water (rather than tap water).

❷ 用完餐後，別忘了清理桌面及清洗碗盤。

Once you have finished eating, don't forget to clear the table and do the dishes.

❸ 今天輪到你洗碗。

It's your turn to do the dishes.

❹ 請用海綿清洗玻璃杯，用刷子刷洗其他的餐具。

Please wash the glasses with the sponge and the rest of the dishes with the brush.

❺ 我打破了一個杯子，真對不起！

I broke a cup, I'm sorry!

❻ 小心不要被火燒傷了。

Be careful not to burn yourself.

❼ 我把水灑出來了，拿條毛巾 [抹布] 來！

I spilled some water. Get a towel [rag/cloth]!

❷ 你應該要知道

烤箱

　　歐美家庭的烤箱通常比我們日常所使用的來得大，且與瓦斯爐臺是一體的。用瓦斯或用電的大型烤箱擺放在下方，上面放烤架。英國有時也會以 cooker 的說法替代 oven。

洗碗機

　　歐美使用的洗碗機幾乎與洗衣機一般大小，可以容納一～二天份的碗盤。通常在就寢前將餐具放入其內清洗。

冰箱

　　歐美有許多家庭使用大型的 freezer。很多人都是開車前往超級市場，一次購足一個星期或一個月份的冷凍食品。若冷凍室和冷藏室是合而為一時，英國以 fridge-freezer 稱之。

須注意的英語

◎ detergent

洗滌劑的種類繁多,且各自有其名稱。舉例來說,像洗盤子用的洗碗精在美國稱作 dish detergent,在英國則稱作 washing-up liquid。洗衣服用的是 washing powder,洗窗戶用的是 window cleaner。此外還有 polish (清潔木製家具的亮光蠟), toilet cleaner, bathroom cleaner 等。

有時也會直接以商標名稱來稱呼,例如英國的 Jif (kitchen 或 bathroom 專用的清潔劑) 和 Domestos (漂白劑的商標) 等。

◎ kettle

燒開水的水壺若譯成英語的話應該是 kettle,但是在英國 kettle 是指類似電熱水瓶但不具加熱功能的保溫瓶。英國人在沖泡紅茶時,通常只使用剛沸騰的水,而保溫瓶的溫度通常只有九十五度左右,英國人說太溫的水可不能拿來泡紅茶!

cupboard

ventilation f[an]

dish draine[r]

kettle

pots and pans

sieve

wok

stiff brush

dish washe[r]

kitchen knife

cutting boar[d]

drain

kitchen sink

bler[nder]

dish detergent

ladle

spatula

eggbeater

peeler

microwave oven

cabinet

frigerator

kitchen herbs

garbage can

non-combustible garbage

kitchen garbage

garbage bag

ersized garbage

recyclable garbage

recycling

垃圾

垃圾的處理除了是現今社會的一大問題之外，也是人人日常生活中的一件大事。入境隨俗地配合各個地方收垃圾的不同規定，不僅可以避免與鄰居之間的衝突，更為環境保護盡了一份心力。

Vocabulary

廚餘	kitchen garbage, food scraps
不可燃垃圾	non-combustible garbage, non-burnable garbage
可回收利用的垃圾	recyclable garbage
大型垃圾	oversized garbage (furniture, appliances)
垃圾收集日	garbage day, trash collection day *rubbish day
垃圾桶	garbage can, trash can *dust bin, rubbish bin
垃圾袋	garbage bag, trash bag *rubbish bag
垃圾處理場	garbage disposal area, trash collection area
循環利用	recycling
有機處理	organic treatment, organic disposal
有毒成分	toxic elements
工業廢棄物	industrial waste

📝用英語說說看

❶廚餘在丟棄前要完全瀝乾。

Kitchen garbage should be thoroughly drained before disposal.

☞在美國是直接將廚餘裝入垃圾袋的。因為他們不在水槽裡放置食物殘渣袋，所以廚餘並不會弄溼。

❷請於垃圾收集日當天早上將垃圾拿出來。

Put out your garbage [trash] on the morning of garbage day [trash collection day].

❸大型垃圾的處理是要收費的。

There is a fee for (the disposal of) oversized garbage.

❹玻璃是不可燃的。

Glass is non-combustible.

❺請再循環利用。

Please recycle (this).

Please put this in the recycling bin.

❻燃燒塑膠物品是產生戴奧辛的主要原因。

Burning of plastics is the main cause of the creation of dioxins.

你應該要知道

垃圾處理

　　垃圾的回收在美國雖依公寓或獨立式房屋而有所不同，但大多數的地方需回收時均需撥專用電話提出申請。而且回收的服務是要付費的，只是大多數的公寓已經將這筆費用內含在房租裡。

　　住宅區裡大多會在街角擺放鋪有垃圾袋的大型金屬垃圾桶 (metal can)，且依可燃及不可燃將垃圾做了分類。最近由於循環利用及垃圾減量的提倡，獎勵玻璃、鋁罐、報紙、雜誌等的循環利用。將可以循環利用的垃圾事先先分類好，等到資源回收日時再拿出去。

　　英國的垃圾回收則是全部免費的，但是並不作分類。甚至有的只用超市的箱子混合盛放著玻璃、鋁罐、衣服、報紙等就拿出去了。

車庫拍賣 (garage sale)

　　美國家庭習慣將不需要的東西在當成垃圾丟掉之前，以便宜的價格拍賣處理。因這樣的拍賣大多都在車庫 (garage) 舉行，所以才有了 garage sale 的名稱。將堆積在家中多餘的東西或舊貨，例如孩子們的毛衣以三件五十美分等便宜的價錢出售。當然，其中還是會有相當好的東西，讓購買的人也能樂在其中。有關這方面的消息通常張貼在超級市場或街角一隅，大家都可以很輕鬆的前往尋寶。類似的拍賣活動還有 yard sale (庭院拍賣)、moving sale (搬家拍賣) 等。英國有時也將這種拍賣稱作 car boot sale。

☺ 須注意的英語

◎ garbage

「垃圾」的一般用語為 garbage，美國所使用的 trash 雖然也具有相同的意義，但是 trash 的用法較偏向口語 (informal)。在英國則使用 rubbish 來指垃圾，雖然 dust 的語意較偏向「灰塵」而非「垃圾」，但是在英國 dust bin 用作「垃圾桶」之意。

◎ disposer

正確的寫法應該是 disposal，為 dispose-all 之意。為裝設在水槽內的垃圾處理器，能將廚餘絞碎，隨水流沖走的設備，在美國的家庭中非常常見。

浴室

西風東漸的結果改變了傳統住宅的樣式，其中最巨大的變革大概就是「浴室」吧！將原本各自分離的廁所與浴室合而為一，改變了在木桶中泡澡的習慣。對於習慣沖澡的歐美人來說，恐怕連享受溫泉的方式也與我們大異其趣呢。

Vocabulary

浴缸	(bath) tub
毛巾架	towel rack, towel ring, towel bar, towel rail
浴簾	shower curtain
	☞ 吊掛浴簾的橫桿稱作 curtain rod。
蓮蓬頭	shower head
浴室清潔	cleaning the bath
去黴劑	mold [*mould] remover
體重計	(bathroom) scales
浴鹽／沐浴精油／ 泡泡沐浴劑	bath salts, bath oil, bubble bath
洗背的長柄刷	back brush, back scrubber
置衣籃	clothes basket, hamper *linen basket
防滑墊	non-skid [non-slip] mat (橡膠製的墊子) tub mat
防滑安全扶手	grab bar

用英語說說看

❶ 請把你的髒衣服放到置衣籃中。
Put your dirty clothes in the clothes basket [hamper].

❷ 天哪！我的體重又增加了。
Oh no! I've gained weight again.
Oh no! I've put on weight again.

❸ 這支洗背用的長柄刷真是太棒了。
This back scrubber is really great.

❹ 把浴缸中的水放掉。
Let the water out of the (bath) tub.

❺ 為了小孩和老人家我準備了防滑墊。
I got a non-skid mat for the kids and the older folks.

shower curtain

back brush

soap dish

shower

toilet tank

grab bar

bath tub

toilet seat

scal

drain

ventilator

towel rack

clothes basket

shaving cream

towel

razor

bath salts

toothbrush

toothpaste

faucet

sink

stopper

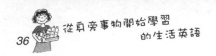

洗臉臺	sink

☞洗臉臺的洗臉槽稱作 basin, washbasin, washbowl。

塞子	stopper, drain plug
洗臉用具	toiletries
牙膏	toothpaste
牙刷	toothbrush
牙刷架	toothbrush stand [holder]
牙線	dental floss
排水管	drain (pipe)
芳香劑	air freshener
除臭劑	odor eater, deodorizer
化妝品	makeup, cosmetics, toilet articles
馬桶	toilet (bowl)
馬桶刷	toilet brush
馬桶座墊	toilet seat
肥皂盤	soap dish
馬桶水箱	toilet tank, *cistern
溫水洗淨馬桶	wash-toilet system
捲筒衛生紙支架	toilet paper holder
生理用品	sanitary napkins [supplies], feminine hygiene

❶ 你想我是不是把我的戒指忘在洗臉臺上了？

Do you suppose I left my ring by the sink?

❷ 隨時保持馬桶座墊的清潔。

Always keep the toilet seat clean.

❸ 浴室裡的排水管似乎阻塞了。

The drain in the bathroom seems to be stopped [blocked] up.

❹ 廁所芳香劑用完了。

We've run out of toilet freshener.

❺ 衛生紙快要用完了。

We're almost out of toilet paper.

❻ 馬桶堵塞住了。

The toilet's stopped up.

❼ 廁所是家中最令人感到輕鬆的地方。

The toilet's the most relaxing [quietest] place in the house.

你應該要知道

何謂 $1\frac{1}{2}$ 個浴室？

　　full bath 指的是含有廁所、盥洗臺、浴缸的浴室，而 half bath 則是指只有廁所和盥洗臺 (即沒有浴缸) 的浴室。在英美國家，一般家庭至少有一間 full bath 及一間或一間以上的 half bath。$1\frac{1}{2}$ bath 的表現方式指的就是這種擁有一套半衛浴設備的住宅。

沐浴劑

　　bubble bath, bath oil, bath salts 等加在浴缸中用以泡澡的沐浴劑種類相當多。bubble bath 是會產生泡泡的，和 bath oil 一樣同為液狀。而 bath salts 則是粉末狀的。

溫泉

　　英國因為沒有溫泉，所以他們也沒有和他人一起共浴的習慣。在英國西南方的巴斯市 (Bath) 雖然是個溫泉鄉，但因現在的水質不夠潔淨，所以不能使用。溫泉的使用雖然早在 2,000 年前的羅馬時代就開始了，但是由於之後溫泉設施被土石掩埋，直到 100 年前才又重新被發現。

須注意的英語

◎委婉表現

bathroom 是「廁所」的委婉表現，類似的用法還有 restroom, lavatory, the John, outhouse (屋外的廁所), latrine (軍隊用語), the loo (英國最常見的說法) 等。

the loo 的語源，有一說是源自法語的 l'eau (水)，另有一說是源自倫敦的地名 Waterloo，詳情則不得而知。

◎ powder room

「化妝室」。通常位於客廳或玄關附近，供客人使用。在英國是相當古老的表現方法。

◎ medicine cabinet

在洗臉臺上安裝的鏡箱。因為鏡子後的架子多用來放置一些簡單的家庭常備藥，故如是稱之。

客廳

家人一起坐在客廳裡各自所喜歡的椅子、沙發上的景象，是美國舊式電影裡家庭和樂的表徵。但是現在臺灣似乎有越來越多的孩子不是一回家就悶在房間裡，要不就是在客廳入迷地打電視遊樂器，真令人擔心。

Vocabulary

日光燈	fluorescent light
白熱電燈泡	incandescent light bulb
間接照明	indirect lighting
隔間	room divider, partition
沙發	sofa, couch
坐墊	cushion
咖啡桌	(放在沙發前的矮桌子或茶几) coffee table
地板	floor
鋪地的材料	flooring
地毯	(覆蓋整個地板) carpet
	(覆蓋一部分的地板) rug
布	cloth, fabric
吸塵器	vacuum cleaner
除溼機	dehumidifier
空氣清淨機	air purifier

用英語說說看

❶ 間接照明最能撫慰人心。
Indirect light is the most soothing.

❷ 天氣這麼好，我們何不把咖啡桌搬到窗邊？
The weather's so nice. Why don't we put the coffee table by the window?

❸ 自從除去地毯 [榻榻米] 之後，清掃起來輕鬆多了。
Since I got rid of the carpet [tatami], cleaning has been really easy.

用英語說明「榻榻米 (tatami)」、「被爐 (kotatsu)」

Tatami are tightly bound thick straw [grass] mats used as flooring in traditional Japanese houses. The size is standardized and rooms are measured according to how many mats per room.

A kotatsu is a low square table with a heating unit suspended underneath. A thick quilt is placed under the removable top to keep the heat in, and you sit around the table with your legs under the quilt to keep warm.

The old-fashioned kotatsu had a hole in the floor underneath the table in which hot coals were placed. More common nowadays are electric kotatsu with a square, electric heating unit attached to the underside of the table.

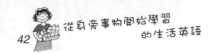

插頭	electric plug
插座	electric outlet, socket
延接線	extension cord
一對二的轉接線	two-prong cord
雙插座的延長線	two-socket plug
兩端有接頭的連接線	two-way plug
一對多的轉接插座	multiple outlet extension
防止電器倒地的裝置	(倒地時自動斷電的裝置) breaker
	(防止倒地的支撐架) stand
觀葉植物	green, *houseplant, pot plant
高傳真、立體聲設備	stereo system
	Hifi (high fidelity 的縮略)
電視機	television (set), TV (set)
落地燈	floor lamp
	*standard lamp
畫	picture, painting
照片	photo, photograph, picture
畫框	frame
書架／書櫃	bookshelf, bookcase
木製的	wooden
壁爐	fire place

❶這套立體音響設備有些特別，不是嗎？

This stereo system is something special, isn't it?

❷那幅畫是不是有點掛歪了？

Isn't that picture tilted a little?

That picture isn't hanging straight, is it?

❸很可愛吧，這是孩子們小時候拍的照片。

They're cute, aren't they? They're photos [pictures] of the kids when they were little.

❹書架上滿是灰塵。

The top of the bookshelf is covered in dust.

❺我的房間是 6 塊榻榻米大的房間。

My room is a six tatami-mat-sized room.

❻木製家具是最好的。

Wooden furniture is the best.

❼請坐。

Please sit down.

Please have a seat.

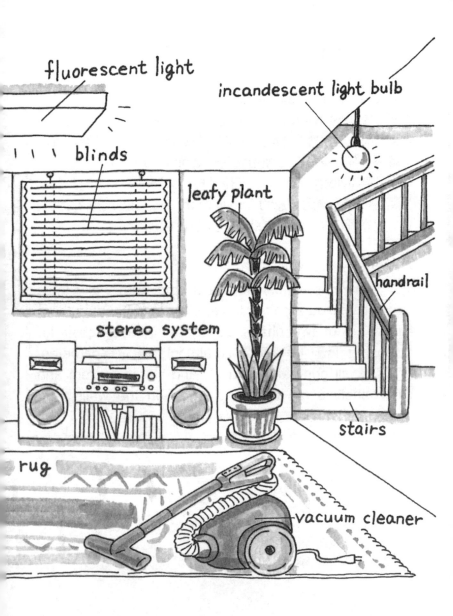

fluorescent light

incandescent light bulb

blinds

leafy plant

handrail

stereo system

stairs

rug

vacuum cleaner

你應該要知道

對家庭而言客廳的意義

在英國 living room 也被稱作 sitting room。和美國一樣，都是全家團聚的場所。有時大家會聚在這裡看看電視聊聊天，有時也會在這裡用餐當作 dining room 使用。有的家庭認為 living room 是專門用來接待來訪的客人，因此另外闢有供家人輕鬆休息的 family room。因為是單獨的房間，可以在裡面做功課、讀書，甚至於睡覺都行。

用英語說明客廳的情形

There is almost always a sofa and a low table (what's called a coffee table) in front of it. Often there is a set of two chairs added or an easy chair for relaxing in. The room is almost always carpeted. There will generally be a TV and stereo system and bookshelves all around, pictures on the walls, and often a fire place.

須注意的英語

◎ coffee table

放在 sofa 前面的低矮 table。放在 dining room 的餐桌稱作 dining room table。若是 kitchen 裡也有擺放餐桌的話則稱作 kitchen table。

◎ solid

整體都是以同一材質做成的家具。例如 solid maple 即指全部都是以楓木製成的。

◎ leaf

為了調整桌子的大小而安裝的木板。drop-leaf table 是指用蝶式絞鏈安裝了可調式木板的桌子。

◎ writing bureau

bureau (政府機關等的「局」) 原義為法語「辦公桌」之意,由此而衍生出 office 的含意。writing bureau 指的是舊式的桌子,桌面是一塊活動的板子,向上翻起蓋起來時外觀就像 cabinet,把桌面放下來就可以在上面寫信或唸書。

◎各式各樣的 board

cupboard 為放置餐具或食物等有門的櫥櫃。sideboard 通常放在餐廳,靠牆擺放,為矮而長的餐具櫥。drain board 則指置放於廚房流理臺旁用以瀝乾餐具的滴水架。

庭院

最近，庭園栽植的流行趨勢已逐漸由提供個人樂趣轉變成也讓路過的人共同來欣賞。的確，把家和外界以高聳的圍牆隔絕開來實在是件令人遺憾的事。

Vocabulary

門	gate
後門	back gate, back door
車庫	garage
後院	backyard, back garden
土壤	soil ☞humus soil (腐植土)。
肥料	(化學肥料) chemical fertilizer
	(有機肥料) organic fertilizer
	(特指動物的排泄物) manure
灑水器	sprinkler
球根	bulb
殺蟲劑	pesticide, insecticide, bug killer
除草劑	herbicide, weed killer
雪鏟	snow shovel
倉庫	(garden) shed, tool shed, storeroom
植物	plant
樹籬	hedge
圍牆、籬笆	fence
露臺	terrace, patio
水池	pond

用英語說說看

❶ 誰在照顧院子的？
Who takes care of the yard [*garden]?

❷ 你的庭院裡總是綻放著應時的花卉。
Your yard [*garden] is always blooming with the flowers in season.

❸ 夏天在院子裡灑水很花時間。
Watering the yard [*garden] in the summer takes forever [a long time].

❹ 最近，栽培花木到處都很風行。
Gardening is in fashion everywhere [with everyone] these days.

❺ 車庫門的運轉不是很順暢。
The garage door isn't working properly.

❻ 灑水器的橡皮水管在那裡，請小心腳下。
The sprinkler hose is there, please watch your step.

❼ 請小心，有球根埋在那裡。
Be careful, there are bulbs planted there.

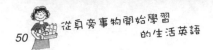
花圃	flower bed, flower border
家庭菜園	kitchen [family] garden, vegetable garden
拱門	arch
藤架	pergola (讓藤蔓植物攀爬的棚架 = arbor)
格子架	trellis (讓藤蔓植物攀爬的格子籬)
吊籃	hanging basket
軟水管	hose
軟水管的管嘴	hose nozzle
鐵鏟	shovel, spade
庭院掃帚	garden broom
樹剪	pruning shears, *secateurs
四腳梯	stepladder
草坪	lawn
割草機	lawn mower, lawn tractor, riding mower, rotary mower
雜草	weed
燒烤架	barbecue grill

❶ 今天天氣不錯。我們來移植花卉吧！

It's nice out today. Let's transplant the flowers.

❷ 把四腳梯搬過來，好嗎？

Get the stepladder, would you?

❸ 在你修整草坪後，把長椅搬開。

After you mow the lawn, move that bench.

After mowing the lawn, could you move that bench?

❹ 草坪生長中，請勿進入。

Grass growing. Keep off.

❺ 小心，那條狗可能會撲到你身上。

Be careful, the dog may jump all over you [may jump up on you].

fence

trellis

terrac[e]

hose

flower bed

backyard

kitchen garden

barbecue grill

lawn mower

lawn

sprinkler

soil

shovel

bulbs

fertilizer

肥料

pesticide

薬

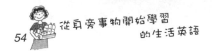

你應該要知道

對圍牆的觀感不同

　　我們有時為了保有個人的隱私權，會將圍牆高高地築起。但是對美國人而言，他們認為住宅應該是開放式的，所以並不會在家的周圍築起 wall 或 fence。對英國人而言，圍牆雖然也有保護個人隱私的含意在，但利用樹籬或木材來裝飾庭園似乎顯得更為重要。英國人傳統上即非常重視庭院，尤其前院是從馬路上一眼就可以看到的，更是費心照料。garden centre, garden show 也很多。

歐式庭園

　　歐式庭園在國內逐漸風行，但相對的，也有越來越多的歐洲人嚮往東方庭園簡樸的風格。相互交流的結果，歐洲也興起了 rockery 風格的庭園。用石頭在庭園的一隅營造出小型的「山景」，並在上面遍植瑞士等山間開放的野花，也別有不同的風味。

須注意的英語

◎ yard 和 garden

在美國，yard 指的是房子周圍用圍牆圍起的庭院。若用 garden 時則表示該庭院經過特別的設計，種植了蔬菜或花木等。但在英國則以 garden 用作庭園的總稱。包括：flower garden, Japanese garden, rock garden, vegetable garden 等。

◎ herb 和 plant

plant 泛指一般的植物。例如 houseplants, pot plants, garden plants 等，大多是小型的植物。herb 則指菜餚中用以增添風味的香料植物。例如 parsley (西洋芹), rosemary (迷迭香), chamomile (甘菊) 等。

◎ terra 的衍生字

terrace 中的 terra 在拉丁語中是 earth 之意。

terrace	臺地
terracotta	赤陶土；赤土陶器；陶俑
terrarium	小動物飼養箱；小植物栽培盆
terrier	㹴犬
territory	領土

雜貨

Do it yourself 的概念是從歐美傳來的。將這些自己動手做的工具或日用雜貨集合在一起販售是相當合乎情理的考量。

Vocabulary

膠帶	adhesive tape
去污粉	cleanser (家具的話則用 polish)
滅火器	fire extinguisher
抹布	dust cloth, floor cloth
蝶式絞鏈	hinge
手電筒	flashlight, *亦作 torch
橡膠手套	plastic gloves, rubber gloves
圖釘	thumbtack [略作 tack], *drawing pin
溫度計	thermometer (「體溫計」亦同)
鋸子	saw
鐵鎚	hammer
釘子	nail
鑿子	chisel
扳鉗	monkey wrench, *spanner
鉗子	pincers, nippers
鉋刀	plane
螺絲起子	screwdriver
錐子	drill

用英語說說看

❶ 你使用去污粉時應該要戴橡膠手套。

You should wear rubber gloves when you are using cleanser.

❷ 為了防止滅火器生鏽，你平日就應多加注意。

In order to prevent the fire extinguisher from rusting, you should look after it on a daily basis.

❸ 把重要的備忘錄用圖釘釘在牆上有助於你不會忘記。

Tacking up [*Pinning up] important memos on the wall will help keep you from forgetting (them).

❹ 體溫計在哪裡？你好像發燒了，何不量量看體溫？

Where's the thermometer? You seem a bit feverish. Why don't we take your temperature?

你應該要知道

維修

　　美國大部分的公寓都有維修服務 (maintenance service) 的系統，當大樓內有用具故障時只要一通電話，maintenance man 就會前來處理。而且清掃工作是由 cleaning woman [lady] 負責的。英國則稱到家裡來幫忙打掃的婦人為 daily help。

通馬桶的用具

　　當馬桶阻塞時，我們會用柄端有個碗狀橡膠吸盤的工具來疏通馬桶。這個工具中文該怎麼說，相信很多人都不清楚，但是英文中它稱作 plunger。

地毯

　　美國或英國的家庭中，房間內鋪上 carpet 是很普遍的，但是清掃起來也特別地辛苦。若不想交由清潔公司而想自己動手整理也是可以的，超市有出借名為 rug shampooer 的機器，只要再購買 rug shampoo 等專用的清洗劑就可以了。

須注意的英語

◎ Scotch tape 和 Sellotape

膠帶的總稱雖然是 adhesive tape，但是大部分的人還是習慣用商品名稱之，在美國用 Scotch tape，在英國用 Sellotape。

其它還有 double-face tape (雙面膠帶), heavy-duty tape (耐用膠帶) 等。

◎ dust cloth

類似的工具還有 duster (擦乾用的抹布；撢子), dust mop (拖把), feather duster (羽毛撢子), rag (碎布), rug beater (拍打地毯的用具) 等。

◎ hoover

指吸塵器，源於製造者的名字 Hoover。

◎ compactor

將家庭中所製造的垃圾壓縮後裝入袋子的機器。

屋外篇

購物

週末的時候家人齊聚，一起前往採購食品、日用品的美式生活方式是充滿互動的。隨著生活方式的逐漸改變，選擇上述生活方式的國人亦日益增多。這也是一種計劃性地避免浪費、即使量少也不買貴的合理態度的學習。

Vocabulary

賣場	department
通道	aisle
貨架	shelf
隊伍	line, *queue
一次購足	the week's shopping
	buy in bulk, bulk buying
	☞英國有社區共同採買的 bulk buy club。
衝動購物	impulse buy
拍賣	sale
特價品	bargain
	☞四處尋找特價品的人稱作 bargain hunter。
	good buy, a find
清倉大拍賣	clearance sale
超低價回饋顧客商品	come-on ☞源自為「吸引顧客前來」而推出特惠商品。
	*loss leader
售罄	sold-out

用英語說說看

❶ 那個產品和即食調理包是在同一條通道上。

That product is in the same aisle as the boil-in-the-bag foods.

❷ 請看下方貨架。

Please look on the lower shelf.

❸ 請在這裡排隊。

Please line up here.

*Please queue here.

❹ 我要去採購這星期的東西 ， 讓我們列張必需品的清單吧。

I'm going to do the week's shopping, let's make a list of what we need.

❺ 聽說這東西真的物超所值，所以我毫不考慮就買了。

I was told this was a real bargain, so I bought it without thinking!

❻ 那項產品似乎在清倉大拍賣中被一掃而空了。

It seems that it sold out in the clearance sale.

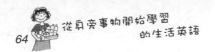
禮券	gift certificate, gift voucher
	*gift token
瑕疵品	defective goods, faulty goods
抱怨	complaint
顧客	consumer
店員	salesclerk, *shop assistant
收銀機	cash register, till
收銀員	cashier
包裝	packaging, wrapping
貨到付款	collect on delivery
	*cash on delivery (略作 COD)
找零	change
換錢	change money
自動兌幣機	change machine, money changer,
	coin machine, changemaker
品牌	brand, brand name
營業時間	business hours, opening hours
合作社	co-op ☞cooperative 的縮略。
收據	receipt

❶ 我給你禮券，請你自己去買一些你喜歡的東西。

I'm giving you gift vouchers, so please buy yourself something you like.

❷ 關於瑕疵品我該到哪裡申訴呢？

Where should I go to complain about faulty goods?

❸ 等候結帳的客人請到這邊的收銀機來。

Any customers who are still waiting, please use this till.

❹ 因為我不久就要使用，所以請簡單包裝。

I'm going to use it straight away, so please keep the wrapping simple.

❺ 可以給我收據嗎？

Could I have a receipt?

你應該要知道

英國人的購物習慣

英國人採購食物的習慣通常是一次購足，很少有人每天買菜的。通常會採買一個星期左右的份量，買些新鮮的肉、蔬菜等以冰箱保存。牛奶則大部分的人都利用配送到家的服務。

在英國即使是禮物也幾乎不會幫你包裝，也不會像國內一樣幫你把購買的東西一個一個放進塑膠袋內，你必須放在自己的袋子裡，如果忘了帶袋子的話，有時還得花三便士左右去買 plastic bag。

美國人的購物習慣

在美國，有所謂的 blue laws。這項法規源自殖民地時期的新英格蘭地區，規定星期天禁止工作、買賣、跳舞等，英國就有很多商店星期天是不營業的。不過，現在的超市、藥妝店等是否適用於此法規則因州而異。反對該項法規的人亦不在少數。

由於美國幅員廣大，郵購型態遂在此應運而生。透過雜誌或電視購物頻道等方式，無論在美國的任何一個角落都能達到輕鬆購物的目的。現在最大的郵購公司是 Sears, Roebuck and Co.，該公司出版的郵購目錄號稱 "Diapers to Light Planes" (從尿布到輕型飛機) 應有盡有。因此 Sears Catalogue 的頁數超過 1,500 頁，比電話簿還厚呢。

⚘須注意的英語

◎ defective goods
「瑕疵品」在英文裡有許多表現方式。defective goods 泛指一般帶有缺陷的商品。faulty goods 則指製程疏失所產生的不良品。seconds 或是 factory seconds 為次級品，意指商品帶有瑕疵，常被便宜拍賣之意。

◎ sale
在英國，January sales 是一年裡最大型的特賣活動，平常定期舉辦 clearance sale (存貨出清) 的商店也很多。至於「結束營業出清」，美國稱作 closeout sale，英國則稱作 closing down sale。

◎ shopping mall
美國的 shopping mall (英國稱作 shopping centre) 非常受歡迎，集合了百貨公司及各式商店的購物中心，規模大到一天都逛不完，即使待上一整天也不會厭煩。

◎ quick lane
超級市場中通常會為購買少量的民眾設立結算速度較快的 quick lane。例如：express checkout (快速櫃臺), ten items or under (購買十項以內的顧客專用的櫃臺), cash only (付現的顧客專用的櫃臺) 等。之所以會設立 cash only 的櫃臺是因為一次購足的消費習慣使得以信用卡支付的顧客越來越多的緣故。

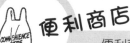 便利商店

便利商店雖然是由美國引進的，但是為了追求方便和快速，早已演變成 24 小時全天候營業以及附加各種便民服務的型態。雖然白天的便利商店熙來攘往，但是深夜的便利商店卻不知怎地帶著淡淡的淒涼。

Vocabulary

二十四小時營業	open 24 hours
送貨到府的服務	(door-to-door) delivery service
新產品	new product
日用品	daily necessities, everyday goods
即食調理包	boil-in-the-bag foods
	☞但在英美相當罕見。
冷凍食品	frozen foods
杯麵	cup-o-noodle, pot noodles
速食麵	instant noodles
零食	chips, cookies, snacks, *crisps
便當	packed lunch, box lunch
果汁	juice
清涼飲料	soft drink
飯糰	rice ball
肉包 [豆沙包]	meat [sweet bean jam] dumpling
電費 [電話費] 帳單	electricity [phone] bill

用英語說說看

❶ 你要把便當溫熱嗎？

Do you want the box lunch warmed up?

❷ 我希望包裹直接送到我家。

I'd like to send this package with the (door-to-door) delivery service.

❸ 大部分的日常用品都可以在便利商店買到。

It's possible to get most daily necessities from a convenience store.

❹ 你回來時順便去便利商店買瓶礦泉水。

Drop into the convenience store and get a bottle of mineral water on your way home.

❺ 電費和電話費帳單也都可以在便利商店繳納。

You can pay your electricity and phone bills at the convenience store.

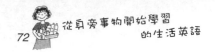

你應該要知道

便利商店

　　英國從很久以前就將便利商店之類的店稱作 corner shop，沿用至今，雖然 corner shop 也是非常常用的語彙，但是，隨著都會區美式的 convenience stores 日漸增多，也會以各家的名稱 (例如 7–Eleven 等) 來替代。便利商店在鄉下並不多，大部分都是 village shop，之後也有許多地方的加油站均更改為商店的型態加入經營。但二十四小時全天營業的比國內來得少，村裡的 village shop 通常和郵局是一體的。

　　即使在美國，便利商店並未像國內發展成多重服務的據點，鮮少提供像送貨到府或代繳水電費之類的便民服務，只是購物的地方而已。而且在售價上既不若超市便宜，產品的種類也比超市少。

須注意的英語

◎ box lunch

英文中的 bag lunch, packed lunch 通常指 sandwiches 之意，若要特別說明中文的「便當」之意時，最好用 box lunch 較好。在英國 packed lunch 一般指有三明治、點心和水果的午餐。但是，野餐時所帶的午餐則以 picnic lunch 或 picnic hamper 稱之。

◎ potato chips

英美在點心方面使用的單字有許多不同。例如：「洋芋片」英國用 crisps，美國用 potato chips；「糖果」英國用 sweets，美國用 candies；「小餅乾」英國用 biscuits，美國用 cookles；而美國的 biscuits 指的是「小型的圓麵包」。

◎ TV dinner

國內便利商店裡陳列有許多微波即可食用的冷藏食品，美國早在 1950 年代起即有所謂 TV dinner 一詞產生。有些母親是職業婦女的小孩，或是單身卻因工作繁忙沒空作飯的成人，就會去買 ready-made dinner 回家用烤箱加熱食用。或者在一週一次的採購時買很多這樣的食品冰在冰箱中，需要時再拿出來加熱。因為大多是一個人坐在電視機前邊看電視邊吃，所以就有了 TV dinner 的說法。並帶有孤單地生活、與家人的接觸時間少等含意。

delivery service

juice and soft drink

frozen fo...

box lunch

frozen fo

daily necessities

rice ball

cup-o-noodle

chips

Curry

Curry

Stewed Beef

Stewed Beef

Mea... Ba...

boil·in·the·bag foods

POTATO CHIPS

TATO CHIPS

在年輕人之間特別受到歡迎的莫過於速食。不僅價格便宜速度又快，再加上到處競爭都很激烈，商家莫不絞盡腦汁，以更新的商品、更貼心的服務來招攬顧客。消費者也樂得享受選擇的樂趣呢。

Vocabulary

外帶	take out, *take away
在店內食用	eat in
免下車訂購服務	drive thru (drive through)
禁菸區	non-smoking area [section]
吸菸區	smoking area [section]
漢堡	hamburger, burger
炸馬鈴薯條	French fries, chips, fries
雞塊	chicken nuggets
可口可樂	Coca Cola, Coke
小、中、大	small, medium, large
	☞有時也會用 R (Regular) 表示 M 的尺寸。
兒童餐	kiddie set, children's menu
紙巾	paper napkin, serviette
吸管	straw
無限暢飲	free refill
剛研磨好的咖啡	freshly-ground coffee
牛肉蓋飯	beef bowl
迴轉壽司	conveyer belt sushi bar

用英語說說看

❶ 能否請你給我 1 個起士漢堡、1 包小薯條、5 個雞塊和 1 杯中杯可樂。

Can I have one cheeseburger, one small fries, 5 chicken nuggets and a medium Coke please?

❷ 「內用還是外帶？」「內用／外帶。」

"Is this to eat in or to take out?" "To eat in/To take out."

❸ 「起士漢堡現在正在做，還得稍等一下。可以嗎？」「這 樣的話，我不要起士漢堡，我改點漢堡好了。」

"We are just making the cheeseburgers, so it will take a few minutes. Is that OK?" "In that case, I'll have a hamburger instead of the cheeseburger."

❹ 「你要糖和牛奶嗎？」「請只給我牛奶就好。」

"Do you want sugar and milk?" "Just milk, please."

❺ 這是一家自助式餐廳，所以請在用餐完畢後自行將托盤 放回櫃臺。

This is a self-service restaurant, so please return your tray to the counter when you have finished eating.

❻ 他們的東西都是現做的，所以很好吃，但是也花時間。

They make the food after taking the order here, so it tastes good, but takes some time.

你應該要知道

速食

提到速食的話就自然而然地會想到美國。一點餐就能馬上享用的速食由於具有便捷、價廉、味美的特點，不論老少都非常喜愛。走在美國的街頭，到處都能發現速食連鎖店的蹤影，而且不論世界各地，都能保持製作的風味不變。

最近，英國高速公路上的休息站裡，也新設立了很多速食餐廳。

速食餐廳

速食的種類繁多，較具代表性的有 hamburger (漢堡), fried chicken (炸雞), pizza (披薩), sandwich (三明治), doughnut (甜甜圈), taco (煎玉米餅) 等。其中有許多速食餐廳的規模早已橫跨全球 ，知名的有 McDonald's (麥當勞), Burger King (漢堡王), Kentucky Fried Chicken (肯德基炸雞), Pizza Hut (必勝客) 等。

McDonald's 在美國已成了最具代表性的速食店，美國的俚語中形容「對速食食量特大」便以 mac out 來表示，美國人還暱稱 McDonald's 為 Micky-D's。

須注意的英語

◎ fries

fries 雖然是複數，但是點購的時候會說 one small fries please。意思是 one portion of fries。portion 是一人份。炸馬鈴薯片在美國一般都以 fries 稱之，但在英國只有在速食店裡用 fries，自己在家裡做的或是在超市買的炸好的馬鈴薯片都叫作 chips。因為英國人在漢堡前擺放的炸魚片和炸馬鈴薯片便稱作 fish and chips。此外，外帶的話則以印度菜和中國菜較受歡迎。

◎ diner 和 café

diner 是一種遍布全美的簡餐館，提供一些炒蛋、煎培根、三明治或漢堡等家常的口味，是價格便宜且氣氛輕鬆的餐廳型態。此外，以 cafe 為名的餐廳則提供沙拉、三明治等多樣選擇，份量是大部分國人都能吃飽的量。

辦公室

最近，沒有電腦就無法工作的情形日益增多。情勢所趨，辦公室的樣子及工作的方式也有了改變。工作再也不光是利用一些簡便的工具，而是必須更有效地靈活運用才行。

Vocabulary

提袋	bag
公事包	(硬的) attaché case
	(軟的) briefcase
旅行用的皮箱	(便於攜帶的手提箱) suitcase
	(一個人提不動的大型旅行箱) trunk
訪談行程表	appointment book, schedule, timetable
資料架	shelf for documents
書寫用具	pencils and pens, writing materials
檔案夾	file, folder
便條紙	memo pad [paper]
檯燈	desk lamp, desk light
旋轉椅	swivel chair
訪客	visitor, guest
影印	copy, photocopy
傳真／傳真機	fax, fax machine
碎紙機	shredder
垃圾桶	trash can [basket], *rubbish bin
電子計算機	calculator

用英語說說看

❶ 你可以趕快影印 10 份嗎？
Can you quickly make 10 copies of this?

❷ 我馬上就傳真給你。
I'll fax it to you straight away.
I'll send it by fax straight away.

❸ 李先生 [女士／小姐]，有位王先生 [女士／小姐] 打電話找你。
Mr. [Mrs./Miss] Lee, there's a call for you from Mr. [Mrs./ Miss] Wang.

❹ 會議 3 點開始，所以我會在那之前回到公司。
The meeting is from 3 o'clock, so I'll get back to the office in time for that.

❺ 我桌上亂七八糟，我不知道東西在哪裡。
My desk is in such a mess, I don't know where anything is.

❻ 我們有客人來，所以請你稍微整理一下。
We've got visitors, so could you tidy up a bit, please.

❼ 我明天上班之前順道去赴約，所以會晚點進公司。
I've got one appointment on the way to work tomorrow, so I'll be late into the office.

你應該要知道

名片

在美國，即使和工作上有來往的人初次見面，也不會像我們一樣交換彼此的名片。因此，對於初次見面的人，一定得努力記住對方的名字並仔細確認其姓名的拼法。

私人辦公室

一般美國的公司裡私人的辦公室非常地多。不僅總經理或領導階層的辦公室是獨立的，甚至連股長的職位也配備有個人的辦公室。這或許是因為個人主義興盛的緣故吧！

休閒生活

美國人特別注重休閒生活，不僅工作上採取週休二日制，暑假或聖誕節假期也是大家盡興遊玩的時刻。特別是暑假時，因為學校通常有長達二～三個月的假期，許多人會計劃舉家開車去旅行，尤其是出租的露營車在這段期間根本供不應求，不提早預約的話是訂不到的。

須注意的英語

◎ PC

雖然 PC 是 personal computer 的縮略，但是通常我們只說 PC 而不用 personal computer 的說法。當然，單說 computer 是最清楚的。

近來，工作場合中的電腦用語亦日漸增多，例如 e-mail (電子郵件), e-commerce (電子商務) 等新名詞的產生；也有許多都已經演變成辦公室常用的用語，例如 file, folder, desktop, copy, trash can 等原本都是電腦方面的用語。

◎ photocopier

影印機一般稱作 photocopier。亦作 copy machine, photocopying machlne, copier 等。

◎ fax

fax 一詞雖然源自 facsimile，但是在辦公室裡幾乎不用 facsimile 這個字。若使用 facsimile 時通常表示「複製」、「摹寫」之意。傳真機以 fax machine 表示。

◎ cabinet 和 cupboard

用以保管文件並附有抽屜的金屬櫃稱作 filing cabinet，用以擺放文具的櫥櫃則稱作 stationary cupboard。

電話

由於行動電話的激增，使得電話變得過於方便，也給對方或周遭的人們帶來相當多的困擾。享受便利的同時也應該注意禮節。

Vocabulary

市內電話	local call
長途電話	long-distance call, *trunk call
行動電話	cellular phone, portable phone, mobile phone
電話答錄機	answering machine, answer phone
通訊聲	dial tone, *ringing tone
電話中	busy, *engaged
在線上	on hold
電話插撥	call-waiting
號碼錯誤	wrong number
直撥電話	direct dial phone
代表號	main [central] switchboard, reception
呼叫器	pager, beeper
公共電話亭	telephone booth, *phone box
*	star key
#	pound key, *sharp key

用英語說說看

❶ 我可以借用你的電話嗎？
May I use your phone?

❷ 為了避免干擾其他乘客，請勿 (在列車上) 使用行動電話。
To avoid disturbing other passengers, you are requested not to use mobile phones (on this train).

❸ 請在嗶聲之後開始傳真。
Please send your fax after the tone.

❹ 我在電話答錄機裡留言。
I left a message on the [their/her/his] answering machine.

❺ 我們的電話未登錄在電話簿中。
We're not listed in the phone book.
We have an unlisted number.

❻ 請給我你的聯絡電話。
Please give me a contact phone number.
Please give me a number where you can be reached.

❼ 有緊急情況時，請打我的呼叫器聯絡我。
If it's urgent, please contact me on my pager.

你應該要知道

電話

隨著英國 British Telecom (BT) 公司民營化的腳步，電信業者之間的競爭也日趨激烈，特別是國際電話費在競爭下變得更為便宜。公共電話方面則有 BT, Mercury, Orange 等數家公司在經營，各自有各自發行的電話卡。

美國則不使用電話卡，而以信用卡替代。但是，近來在紐約等地似乎也漸漸開始使用電話卡。

英國的紅色電話亭 (phone boxes) 雖然很有名，但現在幾乎已經消失殆盡。

在英國，緊急電話是 999，撥這個號碼的話會聽到 "Police, ambulance or fire engine?"，如果想詢問詳細的電話號碼可撥 192，要接總機的話則撥 100。

美國的緊急電話號碼是 911，功能等同於我們的 119 及 110。另外，800 則是一個提供了許多便利的號碼，可以免費得到許多廠商提供的服務及資訊。但是，900 則要付費，須注意。

須注意的英語

◎ person-to-person call

「當接線生找到被指定通話的對象後始付費的電話」稱作 person-to-person call，在英國則稱作 personal call。station-to-station call 則指當號碼撥通後不管誰接都開始計費的叫號電話方式。

◎ telephone dialing codes

country code (國碼)–area code (區域碼)–local number (電話號碼)。在英國，區域碼稱作 STD code (Subscriber Trunk Dialing code)。用法如："What's the STD code for Cambridge?" (劍橋的區域碼是幾號？)

英國的 country code 是 44，美國是 1，臺灣是 886。

例：倫敦　　44–171–×××–××××

曼哈頓　1–212–×××–××××

臺北　　886–2–××××–××××

在國內打長途電話時，必須在 area code 之前加上 0，相同地，在英國也要加 0，在美國則加 1。

例：倫敦　　0171–×××–××××

曼哈頓　1212–×××–××××

臺北　　02–××××–××××

學校制度雖因國而異，但各個制度下產生的問題卻有其共通性，助長學歷社會的填鴨式教育也不只是臺灣特有的吧。現今社會階級依然分明的英國，也是徹底實施精英教育的國家。

Vocabulary

學期	(三學期制) term
	(二學期制) semester
定期測驗	regular exam [test]
期末考	final (exam), *end of the term test
補考	supplementary test, retest, *resit
分數	scores, test results, *marks
成績通知單	report card, *school report
獎狀	certificate, award
優秀學生	excellent student
點名簿	(class) register
高 [低] 年級	upper [lower] grade, *upper [lower] form
義務教育	compulsory education
中等教育	secondary education
寄宿學校	boarding school
禮堂	lecture hall, *lecture theatre

用英語說說看

❶ 你不認為一張只有測驗結果的通知單毫無意義嗎？

Don't you think it's meaningless to have a report card that just gives test results?

❷ 他從國中到大學一直都是位優秀的學生。

He has always been an excellent student, from junior high school right through to university.

❸ 為什麼你這麼害怕高年級的學生呢？

Why are you so afraid of students in the upper grades [*forms]?

❹ 臺灣的義務教育只到國中為止。

In Taiwan school is compulsory up until the end of junior high school.

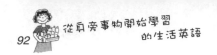

集合同年級學生晨間點名的教室	homeroom, *tutor group
年級	class, grade, *form
畢業生、同學	alumnus ☞複數 alumni。
同學會	(組織) alumni association
	(聚會) reunion
畢業紀念冊	graduation album
在學生	(大學生) undergraduate
	(研究生) graduate, *postgraduate
學費	school fees
	(大學) tuition fees
註冊費	registration fee
捐款	donation, contribution
作弊	cheating
請假單	absence note
曠課	truancy
	☞曠課的學生 truant。
一對一面談	personal interview [meeting], one-to-one meeting, individual conference
家長會	parents' evening [conference, discussion]

❶ 我看了畢業紀念冊之後才知道他和我是同年級的。
The first time I realized that he was in the same grade [year/form] as me was when I looked at my graduation album.

❷ 看樣子明年學費要調漲了。
It looks like tuition fees are going to be raised next (school) year.

❸ 這所學校以除了註冊費之外還要求高額捐款聞名。
That school is well-known for demanding lots of donations on top of the registration fee.

❹ 我作弊被抓到了。
I was caught cheating.

❺ 如果你再繼續曠課下去，就連補考也救不了你。
If you carry on missing school [playing truant], then even resitting the exams isn't going to help you.

❻ 在下一次和指導老師談過之後，我必須做出最後決定要讀哪間學校。
I have to make a final decision on which school to go to at my next personal meeting with my advisor [*tutor].

❼ 我這次考試成績這麼差，想到要開家長會就覺得很沮喪。
I got such bad marks in the test, I'm really depressed about parents' evening.

你應該要知道

英國的教育

英國的教育體系雖然很複雜,但一般來講基礎教育只有二個階段 , primary school 是從五歲讀到十一歲 , 之後 secondary school 是從十一歲讀到十八歲。但是,由於義務教育只到十六歲為止,所以只唸到十六歲也可以。如果繼續升學的話,十六歲必須考 GCSE (General Certificate of Secondary Education) , 十 八 歲 再 接 受 A Levels (Advanced Level) 的測驗,依據 A Levels 的成績來決定進入哪所大學。

在英國的學校裡 teacher 是一般稱呼老師的用法 。 tutor 則專指大學的教授或級任導師。所以 , 若與教授有面談的時候,會說成:"I have a personal meeting with my tutor."

美國的教育

美國的學校情況各州有所不同 , 但大多都採用 elementary school (小學), junior high school (國中), senior high school (高中) 的區分方式。原則上所有的小學、國中、高中都是公立的,採取學區制且學費全免,一直到高中為止都屬於義務教育。

但在美國沒有國立大學,所有的大學不論是公立或私立都收取相當高額的學費。

須注意的英語

◎ cram school

表示「補習班」的用語。cram 即為「勉強塞入、硬塞」之意。

◎ mock exam

即「模擬考」。在英國，各校在舉行 GCSE 或 A Levels 之前都會自行舉辦的模擬測驗。

◎ streaming

英國幾乎所有的學校均採行 streaming (能力分班) 的制度。成績最優秀的學生分入 A stream，之下還有 B stream 及 C stream。雖然反對此一制度的人相當地多，但還是有過半數的學校採用該制度。此外，也有國文被分發在 A stream 但數學卻在 B stream 的情形。這種制度在美國則稱作 tracking。

◎ academic year

指從九月開始到隔年八月的一學年，在這之中較長的假期有 Christmas holiday (聖誕假期), Easter holiday (復活節假期) 及 summer holiday (暑假)。在英國的話，每學期的期中會有 half term holiday (期中假)，大多是為期一週的假期。

銀行

自 1965 年銀行業啟用電腦開始，連線作業的方式使得銀行業務迅速地拓展開來。我們漸漸地也像歐美社會一樣，變成了不需使用現金，只要有卡片四處都方便的社會。

— Vocabulary —

自動提款機	ATM (automatic [automated] teller machine), *cashpoint (machine)
識別密碼	PIN (personal identification number)
存摺	bank book
戶頭	account
帳號	account number
銀行行員	teller, *bank clerk
提款	withdraw (cash [money])
存款	deposit(cash [a check/money])
利息	interest
活期存款	savings account, *ordinary deposit [account]
定期存款	time deposit, term account, *fixed deposit [account]
支票存款	checking account, *current account
劃撥	transfer

用英語說說看

❶ 我想要開一個新戶頭。

I'd like to open a new account, please.

❷ 在查詢過帳戶餘額之後，我要提些錢出來。

I'll withdraw some money after checking how much I've got left in my account.

❸ 定存的利率有多少？

How much interest is there on a fixed deposit?

❹ 我想填張匯款的表格。

I'd like to fill out a form for sending money.

❺ 我想在今天內把錢劃撥到對方的帳戶裡。

I'd like to make a money transfer that will reach the other person's account by the end of today.

❻ 手續費要多少錢呢？

How much commission do you charge?

❼ 不行！我們再不快點銀行就要關門了！

Oh no! If we don't hurry up, the bank will be closed!

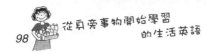

你應該要知道

英國的銀行

英國的情形和美國大致相同,很多時候都不使用現金。除了信用卡之外,還有一種 debit card (亦作 switch card),使用 debit card 的話,會將指定的金額直接由帳戶中扣除。在英國,能夠使用現金的地方大概只有 pub 了。

此外,英國也幾乎不使用存摺。大多由銀行每個月寄送明細表 (full statement) 到家裡來,新推出的服務 telephone banking (電話銀行) 與 electronic banking (電子銀行) 亦廣受歡迎。

美國的銀行

在美國,任何一筆收入都必須到 Security Office (安全局) 去登錄,並會發給一張 Social Security Card (社會安全卡),據此才能在銀行開立戶頭。

須注意的英語

◎ building society

在英國，有 banks 和 building societies 等金融機構。building society 為建屋合作社，專門辦理 mortgage/ home loan (抵押貸款)。和銀行相同，也可以開立一般的戶頭。

◎ borrow 和 lend

要注意 borrow 和 lend 之間的差異。borrow 為「借入」之意，lend 則為「借出」之意。"I'd like to borrow NT$30,000 to buy a computer. Are you able to lend me that much money?" (我想借三萬元買臺電腦，你可以借我這麼多錢嗎？)

◎ plastic (card)

為 credit card 的俗稱。用法如："I bought these shoes on plastic."

◎ personalized check

在美國，只要不是信用破產的人，幾乎都使用個人支票來支付費用，你只要在銀行開個戶頭，銀行就會為你特別製作一本印有姓名及住址的支票簿。

郵局

郵遞信件起源於英國，並在 1840 年發行了第一張稱作 Penny Black 的世界最早的郵票。其後郵政制度便推廣到世界各地，一直蓬勃發展至今。

Vocabulary

郵寄	mail, *post
投遞	delivery
限時專送	special delivery, *express delivery [post]
掛號	registered mail [*post]
(小型) 包裹	(small) package, parcel
郵寄包裹	parcel post
以航空郵寄	airmail
以水陸郵寄	surface mail
郵戳	postmark
郵遞區號	ZIP code, *postcode
郵資	postage [postal charges]
煩請轉交	c/o ～ (care of ～)
存局候領	general delivery, *poste restante
郵政匯票	money order, *PO (postal order)
寄件人	sender
收件人	addressee, recipient

用英語說說看

❶ 星期日及國定假日不送信。
There is no post delivered on Sundays and public holidays.

❷ 請給我 30 美分的郵票 40 張。
Forty 30-cent stamps, please.

❸ 如果我寄限時專送的話，明天會寄到嗎？
If I send this by express post, will it arrive (by) tomorrow?

❹ 我想要將這個包裹以航空保值交寄。
I'd like to send this package by insured airmail.

❺ 如果我將這份郵件以水陸郵寄，你想大概要多久？
If I send this by surface mail, how long do you think it will take?

❻ 以郵戳為憑，請務必在月底前寄出。
Please make sure it is postmarked before the end of this month.

❼ 我要買一張 10 美元的郵政匯票。
Excuse me, may I have a 10 dollar money order?

❽ 不要忘記在寄件人姓名欄內填上名字。
Don't forget to put your name in the sender's box.

你應該要知道

美國的郵遞業務

美國的郵局在入口處都有老鷹的圖形作為標記。如果清楚標示了 ZIP code (郵遞區號)，即使收件人姓名的拼法略有錯誤，通常也能正確地送抵。

除了郵局之外，也有民營的 Federal Express (聯邦快遞) 等，無論要送往國內的任何一個地方，只要一個晚上便能送達，若是國際快捷的話也有 DHL 等。

英國的郵遞業務

英國的郵局有很多都是和便利商店結為一體的，特別是鄉下地方的郵局大多是這樣的型態。

✑ 須注意的英語

◎ correspondents

指「通信的人們」之意。亦有 bad correspondent (懶於寫信的人), good correspondent (勤於寫信的人) 等的表現方式。correspondence 有「書信往返,通信,投信,往返的信件」之意。

◎ esquire (略作 Esq.)

對收件人的敬稱,寫在收件人姓名的後面,如:Richard Smith, Esq.。美國通常只對律師使用這樣的敬稱,但在英國,只要認為對方稱得上 gentleman,即便是對一般人也可使用。有時朋友之間也會用於嘲諷。

◎ fragile

「易碎品」。寫在信封上的用詞還有 Please do not bend (請勿摺疊), Urgent (急件) 等。

◎ postcard

postal card 指政府印製的明信片,而 postcard 則指風景明信片等自行印製的明信片。近來,已不再加以細分,大多通稱為 postcard。

美容院

在美國剪頭髮若期待能有像國內的美髮沙龍般體貼入微的服務的話，恐怕要大失所望了。最好每次去都能清楚地傳達自己的喜好，並將所需服務的內容再確認一次。

Vocabulary

髮型設計師	hairdresser, hair stylist
理髮師	barber
燙髮	perm
剪髮	haircut
吹乾	blow dry
染髮劑	hair color, hair dye
洗髮精	shampoo
潤絲精	conditioner
梳理	hair treatment
分叉	split ends
瀏海	fringe
後面的頭髮	(hair) at the back
後頸	nape
(後頸上的) 髮際	hairline above the nape

♪用英語說說看

❶「喂喂，我想預約燙髮。」
 "Hello, I'd like to make an appointment for a perm."

❷我的髮質非常脆弱，所以不要幫我燙太捲。
 My hair is quite fragile [brittle/weak], so please make it a gentle perm.

❸我今天沒有太多的時間，所以只要幫我剪髮和吹乾就好。
 I don't have much time today, so just a cut and blow dry is fine.

❹你今天要剪什麼髮型?／你今天想把頭髮做成什麼樣子?
 What kind of cut would you like today?
 What do you want done with your hair today?

❺我想要後面剪短，但前面讓它留長。
 I'd like it short at the back, but keep it longer in the front.

❻今年流行蓬蓬的髮型。
 Shaggy haircuts are the in-thing this year.

❼全部完成要花多少時間？
 How much time will it take altogether?
 How much time will it take to finish?

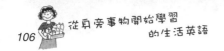
你應該要知道

美髮沙龍

　　在美國，即便在美髮沙龍，也必須另行支付費用的百分之十五左右給美髮師當作小費，在英國則不須支付。此外，若有其他人為你洗髮時，也必須支付二～五美元左右的小費。在美髮沙龍裡可以表明自己需要什麼樣的服務。但是通常洗髮或刮鬍等的服務是另計的。

　　在英國，大部分的美髮沙龍和美容院是分立的。修剪髮型的地方若是不分男性、女性的稱作 hairdressers, hair salon 等。若是顧客僅限於男性的理髮廳則稱作 barber('s)。美容院一般以 beauty parlor, beauty salon 稱之，是指為顧客修指甲、按摩、做臉等的美容中心。

　　通常在理髮廳修剪頭髮時，很多人會順便要求刮個鬍子，但在美髮沙龍裡則不會如此要求。許多英美人對於我們連女孩子都會要求剃淨髮際感到不可思議。

須注意的英語

◎ **appointment** 和 **reservation**

　　appointment 是與 doctor, dentist 或是 hairdresser 等有約時使用的語彙，reservation 則是預約交通工具、飯店、餐廳等使用的語彙。原則上，若是與人約定時間就用 appointment，若 是 預 約 某 一 項 物 品 或 場 所 則 用 reservation 較為適切。例如工作上想與誰約定時間碰面時，可用：I'd like to make an appointment to see [meet] Mr. Smith.

◎ **haircut** 的英語表現

Just take a little bit [a couple of centimeters] off the ends, please. (請幫我剪一點點 [2 公分] 就好。)

Just neaten it up a little bit, please. (請幫我修齊就好。)

I want a radical change, do what you like with it! (我想來個徹底的改變，隨你設計！)

Do you think it would suit me shorter? (你覺得剪短些較適合我嗎？)

I want something feminine [fashionable/different/striking]. (我想要較為女性化的 [流行的／有些不同的／引人注目的] 髮型。)

I want a style that is easy to look after. (我想要剪一個比較容易整理的髮型。)

道路

隨著車輛的日益增多，雖然生活變得相當方便，但是為都市所帶來的弊害也越來越大。大家對從早到晚的交通阻塞、層出不窮的交通事故想必也感到厭煩吧。

Vocabulary

十字路口	intersection, *junction
	☞(T 字路) T intersection
	(三叉路) Y intersection
交通號誌	traffic light, traffic signal
交通阻塞	traffic jam, congestion
一輛接著一輛的擁塞	bumper-to-bumper traffic
繞路	detour, diversion
單行道	one-way street
死胡同	dead-end street, blind alley
平交道	railway crossing, level crossing
斑馬線	pedestrian crossing, zebra crossing
轉彎	curve
	☞blind curve 前方視野不佳的轉彎。
(道路的) 邊石	curb
護欄	guardrail
緊急煞車	emergency stop, sudden stop

用英語說說看

❶ 請在下個路口右轉。
Please turn right at the next intersection [*junction].

❷ 這個時候交通非常擁擠,所以我決定搭火車去。
Traffic is terrible at this time of day, so I'm going to go by train.
There'll be traffic jams at this time of day, so I've decided to go by train.

❸ 我誤闖進一條死巷,很難倒車出來。
I went into a dead-end road by mistake and had real trouble getting out again.

❹ 下一個轉彎不僅非常陡峭,前方的視野亦不佳。
The next curve is not only very steep, but visibility is poor as well.

❺ 我誤把車子開上了人行道的邊石。
I went up onto the curb by mistake.

❻ 小心開車的時候不要睡著了。
Be careful not to fall asleep at the wheel.

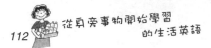

幹線道路	main road
環狀道路	beltway, belt line
	*ring road
高速公路	(只能從設定的交流道進出) freeway
	(也有與一般道路交會的時候) expressway
	(連結州與州的高速公路) interstate highway
	*motorway
交流道	ramp, *slip road
出口	exit
匯流點	junction
收費道路	toll road
收費站	toll gate
行車距離	distance between cars
分叉口	fork (in the road)
最高速限	speed limit
中央分隔帶／ 安全島	highway divider strip, traffic island
中央分隔線	center divider line
車道	lane
超車車道	passing lane, overtaking lane
優先道路	priority lane, right of way
交通訊息	traffic information, traffic news

❶ 在遇到環狀道路前，一路往前開就可以了。
Just keep driving until you come to the ring road.

❷ 我們在下個出口下高速公路吧。
Let's get off the freeway [*motorway] at the next exit.

❸ 在高速公路上亂丟垃圾會被罰款。
There's a fine for littering the freeway [*motorway].

❹ 變換車道時要小心。
Take care when changing lanes.

❺ 這裡是左側 [右側] 通行。
Keep to the left [right] here.
Traffic goes on the left [right] here.
Drive on the left [right] here.

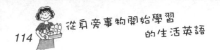

停車場	parking lot, *car park
違規停車	parking violation, illegal parking
拖吊車	wrecker, tow truck, *breakdown truck
交通標誌	road signs
交通規則	traffic regulations
交通違規	traffic violation, traffic offense
計分扣點制度	demerit point
罰款	fine
酒醉駕車	drunk driving,
	driving under the influence
	☞為 influence of alcohol 之意，但通常省略。
酒精濃度測試	breath test
超速	speeding
魯莽行車	reckless driving
無標誌的巡邏車	unmarked police car
正面相撞	frontal collision, head-on crash
駕駛執照	driver's license, *driving license
學習駕照	learner's permit, temporary license,
	*provisional license
吊扣駕照	suspended license, *driving ban
車體檢查	auto(mobile) inspection,
	*MOT (Ministry of Transport test)
汽車保險	car insurance

❶因為停車場裡沒有空位，所以我把車暫時停放在路邊。
There were no spaces in the parking lot [*car park], so I
parked temporarily on the street.

❷如果你把車停在那邊，很快地拖吊車就會把你的車拖走
了。
If you park there, it won't be long before the tow truck
comes to take your car away!

❸你要知道即使只喝一杯啤酒都算酒醉駕駛。
Even one beer counts as drunk driving, you know.

❹他以每小時 100 公里的速度胡亂開車，並當場死亡。
He was driving recklessly at 100 kilometers per hour,
and died instantly.

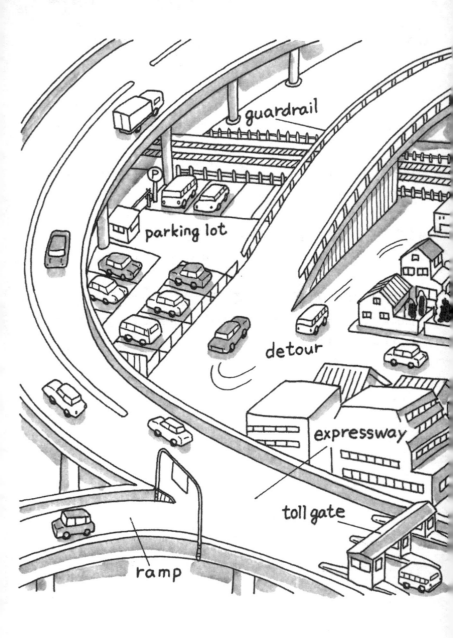

guardrail

parking lot

detour

expressway

toll gate

ramp

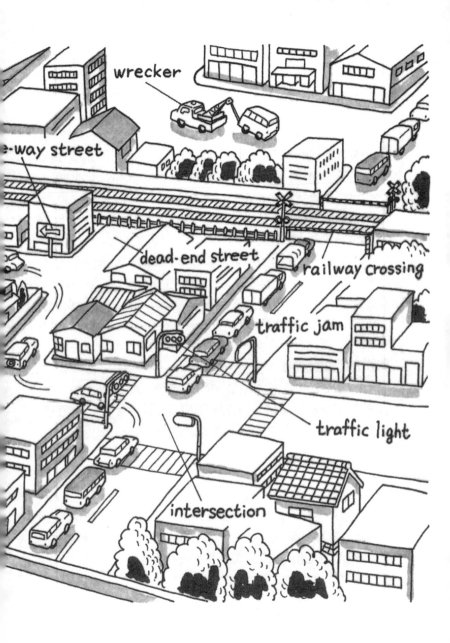

你應該要知道

免下車服務

美國是個無車寸步難行的社會，因此，除了坐在車內就可以購買餐點的餐廳之外，也發展出許多不用下車就可以把事情辦好的地方，諸如：drive-in post office, drive-up mailbox, drive-in theater, drive-up telephone 等。此外，或許很難令人置信，他們連 drive-in bank 和 drive-in church 等都一應俱全。

在英國，因為對大眾運輸工具不滿的人很多，「電車太貴了！」「公車班次太少了！」「老是誤點！」之類的抱怨常有耳聞，因此，英國漸漸地自行開車的人越來越多，drive-through 型態的商店也如雨後春筍般崛起。

英國的汽車保險

在英國，為汽車加保是強制的義務。通常為包含一般性損害的汽車全險及第三責任險等兩種。第三責任險比全險便宜得多。保費也因車型及車齡的不同而有所差異。

緊急救援

在美國，汽車在道路上發生緊急狀況時，可向 AAA (American Automobile Association) 尋求緊急救援。若在英國，AA (Automobile Association), RAC (Royal Automobile Club) 等也可提供類似的服務。

須注意的英語

◎ car pool

在美國，為了節約能源或減緩塞車的情況，通常會在上班等時段實施「汽車共乘制度」。英國則通常不這麼做，大概只有送孩子上學的媽媽們才會結伴同行。

◎ amber light

指「黃燈」。amber 為「琥珀」之意，此說法源於其顏色。

◎ crossing

pedestrian crossing 指「有紅綠燈的行人穿越道」。zebra crossing 則指「沒有紅綠燈，但畫有斑馬線的行人穿越道」，雖然沒有紅綠燈，但通常會有橘色的燈，以提醒駕駛人會有行人穿越。

◎ intersection

在英國不用 T intersection 或 Y intersection 的方式來表示，他們把 Y intersection 比作「叉子」，而稱其為 fork in the road 或 forked road 等。

◎ roundabout

英國的道路特徵為 roundabout (圓環) 特別多。也正因為如此，交通號誌非常少。roundabout 的繞行原則是「全部向右轉」。圓環在美國則稱作 rotary。

汽車

車子簡單的保養或維修其實都是可以自己動手做的。雖然修車廠到處都有，但是人工的費用很貴。所以就算千辛萬苦買到一臺便宜的車，花在維修保養的費用卻是難以避免的。

Vocabulary

方向盤	(steering) wheel
油門 (踏板)	accelerator (pedal)
煞車 (踏板)	brake (pedal)
手煞車	hand brake
喇叭	horn
安全氣囊	airbag
轉向指示燈	turn signal, indicator
耗油率	(gas) mileage, miles per gallon, fuel consumption, fuel economy
汽油	gasoline (略作 gas), *petrol
高辛烷值汽油	high octane fuel
爆胎	flat tire (略作) flat, *puncture
汽車修理廠	auto repair (factory), *garage
打滑	skid
配備	equipment, features, options
維修	tune up, maintenance
小型車	small car, compact car

🕐用英語說說看

❶最近,引擎不容易發動。

It's hard to get the car started these days.

Recently, the engine hasn't been starting very well.

Recently I have had problems starting the engine.

❷你的轉向指示燈還亮著。/你忘了關轉向指示燈了。

Your turn signal is still on.

You've left the indicator on.

❸日本車以省油而聞名。

Japanese cars are well known for getting good mileage.

Japanese cars are known for their low fuel consumption.

❹加滿高辛烷值的汽油。

Fill it up with high octane gasoline [*petrol].

❺有許多人無法自行修理爆胎。

There are a lot of people who can't deal with a flat tire [*puncture] by themselves.

❻你應該讓你的車子一年做一次完整的檢查。

You should put your car in for a full service once a year.

❼因為是小型車,所以操縱起來非常靈巧。

It's a small car, so it's easy to maneuver [*manoeuvre].

你應該要知道

車檢

英國的車檢每年舉行，簡稱為 MOT (Ministry of Transport test)。車檢的費用相當便宜，但若有必須修理的地方時則得修理後再度接受檢驗 。 因為修車廠的競爭很激烈，所以也有很多修車廠提供再次檢驗免費的優惠服務。新車在剛開始的三年內是不需接受車檢的。美國則因州而異，例如紐約州強制規定一年有檢查一次的義務，但在加州則沒有車檢制度。

執照

在美國，通常十六歲以上就有資格取得駕駛執照。因為美國的生活不可一日無車，所以不管是老人家或不擅於開車的人都得被迫上路。因此，交通事故也特別地多。

中古車

在美國買車時，若要購買中古車 (used car) 也可利用報紙或雜誌上個人刊登的廣告。若要購買新車則須向特約代理商購買。

在英國，中古車也稱作 secondhand car。

🕐 須注意的英語

◎ gasoline

　　汽油在美國稱作 gasoline，亦可簡稱為 gas，但在英國則稱作 petrol。加油站在美國稱作 gas station，到了英國則稱作 petrol station。還有，幾乎所有的加油站都是 self-serve (自助式) 的。

◎ garage

　　在英國，garage 有二種含意。一是「車庫」，一是「汽車修理廠」。正確的語意可依上下文判斷。例如：I'm going to put the car in the garage overnight. 和 I need to take my car to the garage to get the brakes fixed.

◎ stoplight

　　American English 中表示「紅燈」之意。

◎ rearview mirror

　　指「後照鏡」之意。

◎ camper

　　露營車，大型的露營用拖車。車裡一應俱全就宛如可以自由移動的家一般。也有很多人租借專供露營車停放的場地，以便定居其中。車裡不僅有寢室，就連廚房、浴室、廁所等也一應俱全，最適合長期旅行了。在英國也稱作 camper van 或 caravan。

交通工具

十九世紀初起源於英國的火車，推動了近 200 年來產業的進步並創造了歷史。隨著鐵路的發展，巴士、飛機的四通八達，世界變得越來越小了。

地下鐵	subway, *underground, (倫敦的地下鐵稱作) the Tube
高架鐵路	elevated railway, EL (elevated 的縮略), *overhead railway
自動售票機	automatic ticket machine
剪票	examine [inspect] tickets
剪票口	ticket gate, *ticket barrier
補票處	fare adjustment station
定期票	commuter pass, *season ticket
行李架	luggage rack
吊環	strap
換車	change trains [buses, etc.]
時刻表	timetable, schedule
佈告欄	notice board
市公車	municipal bus
公車站	bus stop
計程車招呼站	cab stand, *(taxi) rank

🌀用英語說說看

❶購買定期票時，有時需要用到照片。

You sometimes need a photograph to get a commuter pass [*season ticket].

❷行李架上有一個可疑的包裏。

There's a suspicious package on the luggage rack.

❸去高雄在這裡換車。

Change here for Kaohsiung.

❹日本的大眾運輸都很準時，不是嗎？

Public transport in Japan is always right on schedule, isn't it?

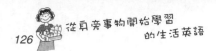

快車	express (train)
臥舖車	sleeping car
餐車	eating car, dining car
普通車	second class car
貨車	freight wagon, freight car
遊覽	excursion
未被預約的座位	unreserved seat
來回票	round trip ticket, return ticket
優待票價	discount rate, reduced fare, concessionary fare
月臺票	platform ticket
中途下車	stopover, *stop en route
長程巴士	long distance bus, highway bus
車掌／列車長	(巴士) conductor (列車) conductor, *guard
團體票價	group fare
兒童票價	child fare
行李臨時寄存處	left luggage
暈車／暈船／暈機	travel sickness
旅遊資訊諮詢處	travel information center
北上列車	northbound train
南下列車	southbound train

❶ 當我旅行時我喜歡輕鬆一點並搭乘臥舖車。

I like to take it easy when I travel and go by sleeping car.

❷ 牛隻被裝在貨車上運送。

The cows were loaded into a freight wagon for transportation.

❸ 進入月臺請購買月臺票。

Please buy a platform ticket to go up onto the platform.

❹ 偶爾在旅途中中途下車也挺不錯的。

Sometimes it's good to make a stopover on the journey.

☞「中途下車」在英式英文裡較常使用 stop en route，若用 stopover 則指「停留一晚再繼續旅行」之意。

❺ 兒童票價是到幾歲為止適用呢？我忘了。

Up to what age are you eligible for a child fare? I forget.

❻ 這藥對暈車 [暈船、暈機] 很有效。

This medicine is really good for travel sickness.

❼ 我確定車站裡一定有為旅客所設置的旅遊資訊諮詢處。

I'm sure there'll be an information center for travelers at the station.

你應該要知道

定期票

美國的定期票有兩種。月票是每個月的一號到月底為止的定期票。另外，也有為期一週的定期票。由於週票的有效日期可自行決定「星期幾到星期幾」，所以在購買之前應詳加規劃，以作更有效地利用。

地下鐵

擁有世界上歷史最悠久的倫敦地下鐵是在 1863 年開始營運的。這條地下鐵有的地段甚至是在深達五十公尺以下的地下行駛，並被命名為 "Metropolitan"(「倫敦的、首都的」之意)。之後，以巴黎為首，歐洲各城市的地下鐵紛紛採用相同的名字 "Metro"。 現在， 地下鐵在英國一般用 underground 這個字，倫敦的地下鐵則因其形狀以 tube 命名， 在英國 subway 指的是「地下道」。美國的波士頓在 1898 年通車的地下鐵以 subway 稱之，在美國，「地下道」用的是 underpass 這個字。

須注意的英語

◎ **compartment**

　　用英語說明的話，即指 separate area of train to seat a certain number of people。

◎ **no-show charge**

　　在美國，對於事先預定座位的乘客，若未接獲取消的通知而不到場，所施以的罰金。

◎ **meal stop**

　　這是美式風格濃厚的用語。指「長程的巴士為了讓乘客用餐而途中停車」。

飛機

隨著世界各地的交流日益頻繁，航空運輸的需求量亦激增。不僅世界各地的連結需要空中運輸，連在國內想要更快地飛到目的地也靠飛機運送。有了飛機，連大家渡假的方式也連帶地起了變化。

Vocabulary

單程機票	a one-way plane ticket
來回機票	a round-trip plane ticket
	*return air ticket
航空運費	air fare
登機證	boarding pass
手提行李	hand baggage
	☞英國的話則用 hand luggage。
隨身行李	carry-on baggage [*luggage]
	check-in baggage [*luggage]
登機手續	boarding procedure
入境手續	immigration formalities
通關手續	customs formalities
座位間的通道	aisle ☞在英國大多使用 gangway。
機艙服務	in-flight service
國際換日線	(the) international date line
時差	time difference
時差不適	jet lag

用英語說說看

❶ 在暑假期間航空運費較昂貴。

Air fares are expensive during the summer holidays.

❷ 請每個人帶入機艙的隨身行李勿超過 1 件。

Please don't take on more than one piece of hand baggage [*luggage] each.

❸ 請在登機前 1 個小時到航空公司辦理登機手續的櫃臺集合。

Please gather at the check-in counter one hour before boarding time.

❹ 入境非歐盟國家非常花時間。

It takes a long time to go through Immigration into non-EU countries.

❺ 請給我靠通道的座位。

Please give me an aisle seat.

❻ 我決定這家航空公司是因為它的機艙服務很不錯。

I decided on this airline because the in-flight service is so good.

❼ 我還沒調適好時差。

I haven't got over my jet lag yet.

你應該要知道

美國的機場

　　美國的任何一個機場規模都很大而且業務繁忙。因為國土非常寬廣，交通運輸有蠻大的比重須仰賴飛機，所以跑道、航站大廈都設計得特別寬敞。也正因為如此，轉機時更須要注意，因為即使是在同一個機場內，有時候還是需要再轉搭巴士或單軌電車到另一邊去，這是相當耗時的。

　　世界上旅客進出量最多的機場是美國伊利諾州的 Chicago-O'Hare 機場，其次是德州的 Dallas-Ft. Worth 機場，而倫敦的 Heathrow 機場則排名第三。

機艙服務

　　飛行美國國內線的飛機是全線禁菸的。此外，有些往返於地方都市的小型飛機，還會詢問乘客的體重。

　　目前，"No frills" (無機艙服務) 的低票價廣泛受到乘客的好評。frill 的原義是衣服的「荷葉邊」，換言之，no frills 即指沒有多餘的服務之意。最近，似乎連英國航空公司飛歐洲的航線上也開始採用 no frills 的銷售策略。

須注意的英語

◎ lounge

　　航站大廈的出入境大廳，英文中以 lounge 稱之。「出境大廳」說成 Departure Lounge，「入境大廳」說成 Arrival Lounge。附帶一提，lounge 的原義為「休憩的場所」，被引用為出入境大廳，或許是因為民族性的不同吧。

　　此外還有 Waiting Lounge, Business Lounge, VIP Lounge, Transit Lounge 等用法。通常醫院的「候診室」稱作 waiting room。

◎ return trip 和 round trip

　　return trip 在英國是指「包含去程與回程的一趟旅行」，但在美國卻是指「一趟旅行的回程」，意義不同須特別注意。在美國若要指「包含去程與回程的一趟旅行」則用 round trip。

◎ coach class

　　「經濟艙」通常稱作 economy class。但是美國的國內航空也使用 coach class 的說法。

旅館

隨著工商業的日益發展，旅館的配備亦越來越先進。旅館的存在不僅滿足了旅客睡眠及飲食的需求，更提供了生命及財產的保護，使得人們能旅居外地安全無虞。一趟愉悅的旅行，舒適安全的旅館是絕對必要的。

Vocabulary

住房手續	check-in
退房手續	check-out
櫃臺	front desk, *reception (desk)
大廳	lobby, *foyer
門房	(負責搬運行李的服務生) porter
	(提供寄物或協尋的服務生)
	*page, bellboy (較年長則稱作 bellman)
預約	reservation, *booking
貴重物品保管 (箱)	safety deposit (box)
電話鬧鈴服務	wake-up call
套房	suite ☞不加 room。
接送服務	(free) pick-up service,
	airport to hotel pick-up service
帳單	bill, account
服務費	service charge
取消費	cancellation fee
小費	tip (left on the pillow),
	pillow money
住宿設施	overnight accommodation

用英語說說看

❶ 我們什麼時候要進飯店辦理住房手續？
What time should we check in?

❷ 我們的退房時間可以延後嗎？
Is it possible to extend our check-out time?

❸ 我已經在 (飯店) 櫃臺留了話。
I've left a message with (hotel) reception.

❹ 我想預訂一間房間，明後兩晚。
I'd like to reserve [*book] a room for two nights for tomorrow and the day after.

❺ 請務必將貴重物品置放於保管箱。
Please be sure to put any valuables in the safety deposit box.

❻ 可以請你明天早上七點用電話叫我起床嗎？
Could you give me a wake-up call at 7 a.m. please?

❼ 一間房間住宿一晚加上服務費要多少錢？
How much is a room for the night, including service charge?

❽ 一個人住雙人房的話似乎要額外付費。
It seems that there is an extra charge for just one person using a double room.

你應該要知道

hotel 一詞的產生

　　用來表示住宿設施的名詞，歐美除了 hotel 以外，還有較古老的 inn (客棧)，較新式的 motel (汽車旅館)。我們也有飯店、山莊等的用法。

　　inn 這個字是在英國十五世紀初開始使用的，該字所代表的語義就像中世紀的住宿設施一般，雖然規模不大但卻有著家庭般的溫馨氣氛，因此現在仍然被愛用。

　　hotel 這個字在英國及美國的逐漸流傳約始於十八世紀末～十九世紀初的時期。 該字源於古法語及中世紀法語的 hostel，除了表示住宿的地方之外也有大富豪的宅邸及公共的建築物之意。 隨著之後 hostel 之中的 s 音消失演變成 hotel，才在法語中逐漸成形，並代表著與 inn 不同的語義，為近代化高級的住宿設施之意。

　　此外，美國有些大型的飯店，為了強調該飯店也有讓客人賓至如歸的溫馨感，在飯店名稱中加入 inn 的也不少。

B & B

　　英國有很多 B & B (Bed and Breakfast) 型態的旅館。其中大部分的 B & B 都是利用一般的住宅，也有的地方和經營者的家庭生活是融為一體的。通常採用附早餐、浴室共用的經營型態。有些價格貴一點的房間，浴室也會設在房間內。

索 引

A

absence note　92
academic year　95
accelerator　120
accelerator pedal　120
account　96, 97, 136
account number　96
addressee　100
adhesive tape　56, 59
airbag　120
air conditioning　6
air fare　132, 133
air freshener　36
airmail　100, 101
airport to hotel pick-up service　136
air purifier　40
aisle　62, 63, 66, 132, 133
aluminum foil　22
alumni　92
alumni association　92
alumnus　92
amber light　119
American plan　141
answering machine　86

answer-phone　86, 87
apartment　2, 3
apartment complex　2, 3
apartment house　2
appliance　28
appointment　105, 107
appointment book　80, 83
arch　50
area code　89
Arrival Lounge　135
assembly room　4
ATM　96
attaché case　80, 83
attic　6, 7
auto inspection　114
auto lock　10
automated teller machine　96
automatic teller machine　96
automatic ticket machine　124, 128
automobile inspection　114
auto repair　120
auto repair factory　120

award　90

B

back brush　32, 34
back door　6, 7, 12, 14, 48
back garden　48
back gate　48
back scrubber　32, 33
backyard　48, 53
bad correspondent　103
bag　80
bag lunch　73
balcony　9
balustrade　6
banister　6
bank book　96
bank clerk　96
barbecue grill　50, 53
barber　104
bargain　19, 62, 63, 67
basement　6
basin　36
bath oil　32, 38
bathroom　39
bathroom cleaner　25
bathroom scales　32
bath salts　32, 35, 38

bathtub   32, 33, 34
bay window   6, 44
bedsit   2
beef bowl   76
beeper   86
bellboy   136, 139
bellman   136
belt line   112
beltway   112
bill   136, 138
biscuit   73
blender   18, 19, 26
blind   6, 45
blind alley   110
block   4
block of flats   2
blow dry   104, 105
board   47
boarding pass   132
boarding procedure   132
boarding school   90
boil-in-the-bag food   70, 74
bookcase   42
booking   136
bookshelf   42, 43, 44
borrow   99
bottle   20
bottle opener   20
bowl   20, 21
box lunch   70, 71, 73
brake   120
brake pedal   120

brand   64
brand name   64
breakdown truck   114
breaker   42
breath test   114
briefcase   80, 82
brush   22, 23
bubble bath   32, 38
bug killer   48
building society   99
building supervisor   4
bulb   48, 49, 53
bulk buying   62
bumper-to-bumper traffic   110
bureau   47
burger   76
burglar alarm   10
burner   16
business hours   64
Business Lounge   135
bus stop   124, 129
busy   86
buy in bulk   62

C

cabinet   16, 27, 85
cab stand   124, 129
cafe   79
calculator   80
call-waiting   86

camper   123
cancellation fee   136
candy   73
canister   20
canned food   20
can opener   20
care of ∼   100
caretaker   4
car insurance   114
car park   114, 115
carpet   40, 41, 58
car pool   119
carry-on baggage   132
carry-on luggage   132
cashier   64, 66
cash on delivery   64
cash only   69
cashpoint   96
cashpoint machine   96
cash register   64, 66
casserole   18
cellar   6
cellular phone   86
center divider line   112
central heating   6
central switchboard   86
certificate   90
chain lock   10
change   64, 66

change buses 124

change machine 64

changemaker 64

change money 64

change trains 124

cheating 92, 93

check-in 137

check-in baggage 132

checking account 96

check-in luggage 132

check-out 137

chemical fertilizer 48

chicken nuggets 75, 76, 77

child fare 126, 127

children's menu 76

Chinese frying pan 18

chips 70, 76, 79

chisel 56

chopping board 18

cistern 36

class 92

class register 90

cleaner 56, 57

clearance sale 62, 63, 69

cleaver 18

cling film 22

closeout sale 69

closet 6

closing down sale 69

cloth 23, 40

clothes basket 32, 33, 35

coach class 135

coat hanger 12

coat rack 12

coat rail 12

Coca Cola 76

COD 64

coffee table 40, 41, 46, 47

coin machine 64

Coke 75, 76, 77

colander 20

collateral 2

collect on delivery 64

come-on 62, 67

commuter pass 124

compact car 120

compactor 59

compartment 131

complaint 64

compulsory education 90

concessionary fare 126

concierge 4, 141

conditioner 104

condominium 2

conductor 126

congestion 110

consumer 64

contract renewal 4

contribution 92

conveyer belt sushi bar 76

cooker 24

cookie 70, 73

cookie cutter 20, 21

cooking knife 18

co-op 64

copier 85

copy 80, 81

copy machine 85

corkscrew 20, 21

corner room 4

correspondence 103

correspondent 103

cosmetics 36

couch 40

country code 89

country home 4

country house 4

country-style 4

cram 95

cram school 95

crisps 70, 73

crockery 20

crossing 119

cunning 95

cupboard 16, 26, 47, 85

cup-o-noodle 70, 74

curb   110, 111
current account   96
curtain rod   32
curve   110, 111
cushion   40, 44
customs formalities   132
cutlery   20
cutting board   18, 26

D

daily necessities   70, 71, 74
damaged goods   64
dead-end street   110, 117
deck   9
defective goods   64, 67, 69
dehumidfier   40
delivery   13, 100
delivery service   70, 71, 74
demerit point   114
dental floss   36
deodorizer   36
department   62
Departure Lounge   135
deposit   2, 3, 96
desk lamp   80, 83
desk light   80
detached house   4, 5

detergent   25
detour   110, 116
dial tone   86
diner   79
dining car   126
dining room table   47
direct dial phone   86
discount rate   126
dish   20
dishcloth   22
dish detergent   22, 25, 26
dish drainer   22, 26
dishrag   22
dishwasher   16, 17, 26
disposal   29, 31
disposer   31
distance between cars   112
diversion   110
Domestos   25
donation   92, 93
doorbell   10
doormat   12, 14
door phone   10
doorplate   10, 11
door scraper   12
doorstop   12
door-to-door delivery service   70, 71
double-face tape   59

double glazing   6
double window   6, 7
down payment   2
drain   22, 29, 34, 36, 37
drain board   47
drainer   20
drainer tray   22
drain pipe   36
drain plug   36
drawing pin   56
drill   56
drinking room table   47
driver's license   114
drive through   76
drive thru   76
driveway   12
driving ban   114
driving license   114
driving under the influence   114
drunk driving   114, 115
duplicate key   12, 13
dust   31
dust bin   28, 31
dust cloth   56, 59
duster   59
dust mop   59

E

eat in   76, 77

eating car   126

e-commerce   85

economy class   135

eggbeater   20, 26

egg whisk   20

EL   124

electricity bill   70, 71

electric outlet   42

electric plug   42

electric pot   18

electromagnetic cooker   16

elevated   124

elevated railway   124, 129

e-mail   85, 103

emergency stop   110

endocrine disrupters   28

end of the term test   90

engaged   86

entrance light   10

entryway light   10, 11

equipment   120

Esq.   103

esquire   103

estate agent   4

European plan   141

evacuation point   4

everyday goods   70

examine ticket   124

excellent student   90, 91

excursion   126

exit   112, 113

express   126, 129

express checkout   69

express delivery   100

express post   100, 101

express train   126

expressway   112, 116

extension cord   42

extractor fan   16

F

fabric   40

factory seconds   69

family garden   50

fan   16, 17

fare adjustment station   124, 128

faucet   22, 35

faulty goods   64, 65, 69

fax   80, 81, 85

fax machine   80, 82, 85

feather duster   59

features   120

feminine hygiene   36

fence   48, 52, 54

ferroconcrete   4

fertilizer   53

file   80, 83

filing cabinet   85

final   90

final exam   90

find   62

fine   114

fire escape   9

fire extinguisher   56, 57

fire place   42

fixed account   96, 97

fixed deposit   96, 97

flashlight   56

flat   2, 3, 120

flat tire   120, 121

flight   9

floor   40

floor cloth   56

flooring   40

floor lamp   42

flour   19

flower arrangement   12

flower bed   50, 52

flower border   50

fluorescent light   40, 45

foil   22

folder   80

food processor   18

food scraps   28
fork   112
forked road   119
fork in the road   112, 119
form   92, 93
foyer   136
fragile   103
frame   42
free pick-up service   136
free refill   76
free-standing house   4, 5
freeway   112, 113
freezer   14, 16, 17, 24
freight car   126
freight wagon   126, 127
French fries   75, 76
freshly-ground coffee   76
fridge   16, 17
fridge-freezer   24
fries   76, 77, 79
fringe   104
front   141
frontal collision   114
front desk   136, 138, 141
front door   14
front stairs   10
front steps   10, 15
frozen food   70, 74

fruit knife   18, 19
frying pan   18
fuel consumption   120, 121
fuel economy   120
furnished   2
furniture   28

G

gangway   132
garage   2, 10, 48, 120, 123
garbage   31
garbage bag   27, 28
garbage can   22, 27, 28
garbage day   28, 29
garbage disposal area   28
garden   49, 55
garden broom   50
garden shed   48
gas   16, 120, 123
gas burner   16
gas mileage   120
gasoline   120, 121, 123
gas station   123
gate   10, 11, 48
gate post   10
general delivery   100
gift certificate   64
gift token   64
gift voucher   64,

65
good buy   62
good correspondent   103
grab bar   32
grade   92, 93
graduate   92
graduation album   92, 93
grater   20
greaseproof paper   22
green   42
group fare   126
guard   12, 13, 126
guardrail   110, 116
guest   80
gutter   22

H

hair at the back   104
hair color   104
haircut   104, 105, 107
hairdresser   104
hair dye   104
hairline above the nape   104
hair stylist   104
hair treatment   104
hall light   10, 11
hall stairs   15
hamburger   74, 76
hammer   56
hamper   32, 33
hand baggage

132, 133
hand brake   120
handle   18
hand luggage   132,
   133
handrail   6, 45
hanging basket   50
head-on crash   114
heating   6
heavy-duty tape
   59
hedge   48
herb   55
herbicide   48
Hifi   42
high octane fuel
   120
highway bus   126
highway divider
   strip   112
hinge   56
home loan   99
homeroom   92
hoover   59
horn   120
hose   49, 50, 52
hose nozzle   50
hot plate   18
house alarm   10
houseplant   42
housing
   development   2
housing loan   2, 3

I

ice tray   16
illegal parking

114
immigration
   formalities   132
impulse buy   62
incandescent light
   bulb   40, 45
indicator   120, 121
indirect lighting
   40, 42
individual
   conference   92
industrial waste
   28
in-flight service
   132, 133
insecticide   48
inspect ticket   124
instant noodles   70
intercom   10, 11
interest   96, 97
international date
   line   132
intersection   110,
   111, 117, 119
interstate highway
   112

J

January sales   69
Japanese style meat
   dumpling   70
jar   20
jet lag   132, 133
Jif   25
John   39
juice   70, 74
junction   110, 111,

112

K

kettle   18, 25, 26
key   9
key money   2
kiddie set   75, 76
kitchen door   6, 7,
   12
kitchen garbage
   27, 28, 29
kitchen garden
   50, 53
kitchen herb   27
kitchen knife   18,
   26
kitchen roll   22
kitchen sink   22,
   26
kitchen table   47

L

ladle   20, 26
landing   6
lane   112, 113
large   76
latrine   39
lavatory   39
lawn   50, 51, 53
lawn mower   50,
   53
lawn tractor   50
leaf   47
learner's permit
   114
lecture hall   90
lecture theatre   90

left luggage   126
lemon juicer   20
lemon squeezer
   20
lend   99
letter box   10, 15
level crossing   110
lid   18, 21
line   62, 63, 67
linen basket   32
liquidizer   18
lobby   135, 136,
   139
local call   86
local number   89
lock   9, 11
loft   6
long distance bus
   126
long-distance call
   86
loo   39
loss leader   62
lounge   135
lower form   90
lower grade   90
luggage rack   124
luncheon mat   22

M

mail   100, 103
mailbox   10, 11,
   15
mail drop   10
mail slot   10
main road   112
main switchboard

86
maintenance   58,
   120
makeup   36
mansion   9
manure   48
marks   90
meal stop   131
measuring cup   18,
   19
measuring spoon
   18, 19
medicine cabinet
   39
medium   76, 77
meeting house   4
memo pad   80, 83
memo paper   80
microwave   16, 17
microwave oven
   16, 27
mileage   120, 121
miles per gallon
   120
milk pan   18
Ministry of
   Transport test
   114
mobile phone   86,
   87
mock exam   95
mold remover   32
money changer
   64
money order   100,
   101
monkey wrench

56
mortgage   2, 3, 99
MOT   114, 122
motorway   112
mould remover
   32
multiple outlet
   extension   42
municipal bus
   124, 129

N

nail   56
nameplate   10, 11
nape   104
new product   70
nippers   56
non-burnable
   garbage   28
non-combustible
   garbage   27, 28
non-skid mat   32,
   33
non-slip mat   32
non-smoking area
   74, 76
non-smoking
   section   76
northbound train
   126
no-show charge
   131
notice board   124,
   128

O

occupant   4

odor eater   36

one-room apartment   2

one-to-one meeting   92

one-way plane ticket   132

one-way street   110, 117

on hold   86

open hallway   6

opening hours   64

open stairwell   6

open   24 hours   70

option   120

ordinary account   96

ordinary deposit   96

organic disposal   28

organic fertilizer   48

organic treatment   28

outbuilding   14

outhouse   39

outside lights   10

oven   16, 17, 24

overhead railway   124

overnight accommodation   136

oversized garbage   27, 28, 29

overtaking lane   112

P

package   13, 100, 101

packaging   64, 66

packed lunch   70, 73, 74

page   136

pager   86, 87

painting   12, 42

pan   18, 26

paper napkin   22, 75, 76

paper towel   22

parcel   100

parcel post   100

parents' conference   92

parents' discussion   92

parents' evening   92, 93

paring knife   18, 19

parking lot   114, 115, 116

parking space   2

parking violation   114

partition   40

passing lane   112

patio   48

PC   85

pedestrian crossing   110, 117, 119

peeler   20, 21, 26

peephole   12

percolator   18

pergola   50

perm   104, 105

personal call   89

personal identification number   96

personal interview   92

personalized check   99

person-to-person call   89

pesticide   48, 53

petrol   120, 121, 123

petrol station   123

phone bill   70, 71

phone box   86, 88

photo   42

photocopier   82, 85

photocopy   80

photocopying machine   85

photograph   42

pick-up service   136, 139

picnic hamper   73

picnic lunch   73

picture   12, 42, 43

pillow money   136

PIN   96

pincers   56

place mat   22

plane   56
plant   48, 55
plastic   99
plastic card   99
plastic gloves   56
plastic wrap   22
plate   20
platform ticket   126, 127
Please do not bend   103
PO   100
polish   25, 56
pond   48
porch   9
portable phone   86
porter   136, 139
post   100, 101
postage   100
postal card   103
postal charges   100
postal order   100
postbox   15
postcard   103
postcode   100
poste restante   100
postgraduate   92
postmark   100, 101
pot   18, 26
potato chips   73
pot noodles   70
pot plant   42
pound key   86
powder room   39
pressure cooker

18
priority lane   112
provisional license   114
pruning shears   50
puncture   120

Q

queue   62, 63
quick lane   69

R

rag   23, 59
railing   6
railway crossing   110
ramp   112, 116
rank   124
razor   34
real estate agency   4
real estate agent   4
rearview mirror   123
receipt   64
reception   86, 136, 137, 141
reception desk   136, 141
recipe   19
recipient   100
reckless driving   114
recyclable garbage   27, 28
recycling   28
redecorate   6

reduced fare   126
refrigerator   16, 27
register   90
registered mail   100
registered post   100
registration fee   92, 93
regular exam   90
regular test   90
rent   2
report card   90, 91
reservation   107, 136
resit   90, 93
restroom   39
retest   90
return air ticket   132
return ticket   126
return trip   135
reunion   92
rice ball   70, 74
riding mower   50
right of way   112
ringing tone   86
ring road   112, 113
road sign   114
rolling pin   20, 21
room divider   40
rotary   119
rotary mower   50
roundabout   119
round trip   135
round trip plane ticket   132

round trip ticket
126
rubber gloves　56,
57
rubbish　31
rubbish bag　28
rubbish bin　22,
28, 80
rubbish day　28
rug　40, 45
rug beater　59
rustic　4

S

safety deposit
136, 138
safety deposit box
136, 137
sale　62, 67, 69
salesclerk　64, 67
sanitary napkins
36
sanitary supplies
36
Saran Wrap　22
saucepan　18
savings account
96
saw　56
scales　32, 34
schedule　80, 124,
125
school fees　92
school report　90
scores　90
Scotch tape　59
scouring brush　22

screwdriver　56
seasoning　20, 21
season ticket　124,
125
secateurs　50
secondary education
90
second class car
126
second home　4
seconds　69
secret code　10
secret number　10
security　2, 10
security deposit　2
security lock　10
self-locking door
10
Sellotape　59
semester　90
sender　100, 101
service charge
136, 137
serviette　22, 76
shampoo　104
shaving cream　35
shed　6, 48
shelf　16, 17, 62,
63, 66
shoe box　12
shoebox　15
shoehorn　12
shoe rack　12, 15
shop assistant　64
shopping centre
69
shopping mall　69

shovel　50, 53
shower curtain
32, 34
shower head　32
shredder　80, 82
sideboard　16, 47
sieve　20, 26
single-family house
4
sink　34, 36, 37
skid　120
sleeping car　126,
127
slip road　112
small　76, 77
small car　120, 121
small package
100
small saucepan　18
smoking area　75,
76
smoking section
76
snacks　70
snow shovel　48
soap　22
soap dish　34, 36
socket　42
sofa　40
soft drink　70, 74
soil　48, 53
sold-out　62
solid　47
southbound train
126
southern exposure
4

south-facing   4
spade   50
spanner   56
spare key   12, 13
spatula   20, 26
special delivery   100
speeding   114
speed limit   112
spice   20
split ends   104
sponge   22, 23
spout   18
sprinkler   48, 49, 53
stairs   6, 7, 15, 45
stairway   6
stand   42
standard lamp   42
star key   86
stationary cupboard   85
station-to-station call   89
STD code   89
steamer   18
steering wheel   120
step   9, 15
stepladder   50, 51
steps   6, 9, 15
stereo system   42, 43, 45
stew pot   18
stiff brush   22
stop en route   126, 127

stoplight   123
stopover   126, 127
stopper   34, 36
storage shed   6
storage space   6
store room   48
storeroom   6, 7
strainer   20
strap   124
straw   75, 76
streaming   95
studio flat   2
subway   124, 129, 130
sudden stop   110
suitcase   80
suite   136
sunny   4
super   4
superintendent   4
supplementary test   90
surface mail   100, 101
suspended license   114
sweet bean jam dumpling   70
sweets   73
swivel chair   80, 83

T

tablespoon   19
tack   56, 57
take away   76
take out   75, 76,

77
tap   22, 23
taxi rank   124
teaspoon   19
tea strainer   20
telephone booth   86
television   42
television set   42
teller   96
temperature control   16
temperature knob   16
temporary license   114
tenant   4
ten items or under   69
term   90
term account   96
terra   55
terrace   48, 52, 55
terracotta   55
terrarium   55
terrier   55
territory   55
test results   90, 91
thermometer   56, 57
thumbtack   56
ticket barrier   124
ticket gate   124, 128
till   64, 65
time deposit   96
time difference

132

time sharing   9

timetable   80, 124, 128

tinned food   20

tin opener   20

T intersection   110

tip   136

tip left on the pillow   136

toilet   36, 37

toilet articles   36

toilet bowl   36

toilet brush   36

toilet cleaner   25

toilet paper   37

toilet paper holder   36

toiletries   36

toilet seat   34, 36

toilet tank   34, 36

toll gate   112, 116

toll road   112

tongs   20

tool house   6

tool shed   48

toothbrush   35, 36

toothbrush holder   36

toothbrush stand   36

toothpaste   35, 36

torch   56

towel   23, 35

towel bar   32

towel rack   32, 35

towel rail   32

towel ring   32

tow truck   114, 115

toxic elements   28

toxic waste   28

tracking   95

traffic information   112

traffic island   112

traffic jam   110, 111, 117

traffic light   110, 117

traffic news   112

traffic offense   114

traffic regulations   114

traffic signal   110

traffic violation   114

transfer   96, 97

Transit Lounge   135

transplant   51

trash   31

trash bag   28

trash basket   80

trash can   22, 28, 80, 82

trash collection area   28

trash collection day   28, 29

travel information center   126

travel sickness

126, 127

trellis   50, 52

truancy   92

truant   92, 93

trunk   80

trunk call   86

tub   32, 33

tube   124, 130

tub mat   32

tuition fees   92, 93

tune up   120

turn signal   120, 121

TV   42

TV dinner   73

TV set   42

two-prong cord   42

two-socket plug   42

two-stor(e)y building   2

two-way plug   42

U

umbrella stand   12

undergraduate   92

underground   124, 130

unmarked police car   114

unreserved seat   126

upper form   90, 91

upper grade   90, 91

Urgent   103

utility room   9

V

vacuum cleaner
   40, 45
vase   12
vegetable garden
   50
ventilation fan   16,
   26
verandah   9
VIP Lounge   135
visitor   80, 81, 82

W

Waiting Lounge
   135
waiting room   135
wake-up call   136,
   137
washbasin   36
washbowl   36
washing powder
   25
washing-up liquid
   22, 25
wash-toilet system
   36
water purifier   22
waxed paper   22
weed   50
weed killer   48
week's shopping
   62, 63, 66
well-lit   4
wheel   120
window cleaner

25
window cleaning
   6
window frame   6,
   42
window shade   6
window washer   6
withdraw   96, 97
wok   18, 26
wooden   4, 42, 43
wrapping   64, 65
wrecker   114, 117
writing bureau   47
wrong number   86

Y

yard   49, 55
Y intersection
   110

Z

zebra crossing
   110, 119
ZIP code   100

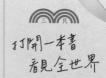

須注意的英語

◎ front desk

飯店櫃臺在英語中雖然使用 front desk 或 reception (desk)，但是辦理住宿登記時通常用 reception，與人相約等候時則用 lobby。"Please check in at reception when you arrive at the hotel." (抵達飯店之時請在櫃臺辦理登記手續。)

◎ concierge

concierge (門房) 這個字雖然是法語，但在英文中亦被採用。其主要的工作是提供客人諮詢及相關的服務。

◎ American plan 和 European plan

在美國，American plan 指「含兩餐的住宿」，European plan 則指「不含餐費的住宿」。